THE
WAHATOYA

THE
WAHATOYA

IN THE VALLEY
OF THE SHADOW

Gary L. Bridges

Copyright © 2008 by Gary L. Bridges.

Library of Congress Control Number:		2008910048
ISBN:	Hardcover	978-1-4363-8331-8
	Softcover	978-1-4363-8330-1

All rights reserved. No part of this book may be reproduced or transmitted in any form or by any means, electronic or mechanical, including photocopying, recording, or by any information storage and retrieval system, without permission in writing from the copyright owner.

This is a work of fiction. Names, characters, places and incidents either are the product of the author's imagination or are used fictitiously, and any resemblance to any actual persons, living or dead, events, or locales is entirely coincidental.

This book was printed in the United States of America.

To order additional copies of this book, contact:
Xlibris Corporation
1-888-795-4274
www.Xlibris.com
Orders@Xlibris.com
55219

DEDICATION

To the memory of Ernie Fognani
January 29, 1960 to August 3, 2007

*A man of many companions may come to ruin, but
there is a friend who is closer than a brother.*
Proverbs 18:24

Prologue

If you're a first-time reader of the Cuchara series, you might want to take a few minutes to read this short section and get caught up on the characters and their stories. Better yet, read *The Cuchara Chronicles*, the first novel of the series, and *Out of Purgatory: The Chronicles Continue.* If you're a faithful reader and just want to be reminded of who's who and their parts in the continuing story, I hope that the next few pages will whet your appetite for what comes next.

The Cuchara Chronicles began the story of Lane Curry and his young son, Steve Curry as they began their new lives in Cuchara, Colorado. Lane's family had put down roots in Cuchara many years prior and he had spent his summers hiking the mountain trails and fishing at Blue Lake and Bear Lake. After the tragic death of his wife, Lane is desperate to shake the malaise gripping his and his son's lives. Lane is a successful author and scholar who gives up a lucrative teaching position at the University of Texas to return to Cuchara. The two eventually settle in at the family homestead, which was originally built by Lane's grandfather, Sven Curry. Even though Steve takes to the rural mountain environment, the darkness of his mom's death still looms between him and his dad.

An unexpected visitor literally "drops in" when a giant Chinook helicopter lands in the ski resort's parking lot one day. An Air Force general strides out from underneath the chopper's giant blades and into Steve's life. General Ben Curtis's son is several days overdue on his hiking trip near Trinchera Peak, which is not far from Cuchara. Steve, now an accomplished horseman and his dad volunteer to help. They and Steve's big dog, Samson, join the search and rescue team. Samson plays a key role in locating the lost hiker. By the end of the mission, Steve comes to grips with the loss of his mom through another tragic and heartbreaking encounter with death and General Curtis becomes a part of Steve's future.

Slowly but surely Lane emerges from his own grief and finds himself in a relationship with a local artist. He struggles with guilt for allowing love to enter his life again and worries about how Steve will react to another woman in their lives. In the meantime, Lane becomes aware of a covert attempt to buy the family property, including the very valuable water rights. With the help of a private investigator, Lane discovers that the mysterious buyer is probably after the family secret that even Lane did not know about. His grandfather Sven, though long dead, becomes a central figure in the ensuing struggle and the ultimate discovery that will literally rock the family.

Out of Purgatory begins when a Spanish priest, one of the Cuchara Valley's first settlers, is scalped and near death at the hands of enraged Ute Indians. The book travels back and forth between the early days of the Cuchara Valley, when the Ute Indians and the first Spanish settlers co-existed, sometimes peacefully and other times not so peacefully, and the present.

In the beginning, Steve Curry and Samson deal with one of many daily problems in Steve's summer job. He has graduated from Fort Lewis College and is working for the U. S. Forest Service managing and maintaining the local campgrounds. Steve and Lane are both still living on the family property. Lane has rejuvenated his academic career at Southern University in Pueblo, Colorado and Steve is deciding what to do with the rest of his life. General Curtis returns in an effort to find solace and looks to Steve to help him. The reunion puts Steve in a perilous position and finds him once again staring death in the face.

A new character, Taylor Youngblood, a full-blooded Ute Indian and classmate of Steve's at Fort Lewis College, enters the story. He and Steve come from very different backgrounds. Taylor was raised on the Ute Indian Reservation near Ignacio, Colorado, yet they share more than they could possibly know. Taylor seeks Lane's help with a potentially devastating financial problem facing the Ute tribe and, once again, Lane calls on his friend, the private investigator, to help. Their search for the truth stretches all the way to Washington, D.C., to North Korea and ultimately to Chaparral Falls, a favorite hide-out of Sven Curry, Lane's long lost grandfather. CIA agents, FBI agents, auditors from the U.S. Comptroller and a casino dot the landscape of espionage and counterfeit bills on the road to resolution. One Curry mystery from the past and one dilemma waiting for the future are solved in this book.

Other new characters include Towaoc, the Ute chief who plays a prominent role in the early years and Father Miguel, the Spanish priest who saved Towaoc's life as a young boy and helped raise him. The Utes set up

THE WAHATOYA

camp in the mountains at the foot of West Peak during the summer months. Miguel and Towaoc, side by side, try to administer their respective tribes while growing to know and respect each other. Their friendship is tested many times as the Spanish settlers are joined by white settlers, including a contingent of Swedes.

Along the way, the book explores the relationships of the Ute Indians and a variety of challenges, some deadly, to the tribe's existence. Towaoc emerges as one of the greatest Ute chiefs. He rides on his first raid against a Spanish wagon train at sixteen years of age and courts his wife-to-be in an unusual and dangerous manner. Towaoc is forced to send his best friend and most trusted warrior to save his wife and daughter from a Spanish wagon train. A deadly encounter between teen-age Ute warriors and unscrupulous Spanish bandits sets the stage for the Ute Indian tribe's salvation in the distant future.

The Milk Run—April 1944

The big engine sputtered then coughed as it valiantly tried to wake up. Its long propellers swung lazily, struggling for momentum in the frigid Colorado air. A startled prairie dog, standing sunrise sentinel for a neighboring colony, barked an alarm and scurried below ground. He poked his head up and scanned the horizon for danger. The big B-24 engine belched a cloud of exhaust with a mighty roar and the propellers spun furiously in a maelstrom of cold air.

Captain Ben Curtis smiled. He never tired of the excitement of starting the giant engines. As soon as the number three engine settled into its ear-throbbing idle (pilots always started number three engine first since it provided power to the plane's hydraulic pump), Ben started the other three engines in turn. The engines' vibration and sound coursed through the plane's airframe. The cockpit crew adjusted their headsets tighter over their ears as they completed the Engine Start checklist.

"Pueblo Ground Control, Tiger One-Eleven is ready to taxi," the co-pilot, Bill Haley, radioed crisply.

"Tiger One-Eleven you're cleared to taxi runway three-five. Winds are two-seven-zero at eight knots. Altimeter setting is two-niner-eight-five. You're number one for take-off."

Ben eased the throttles forward and the B-24 lumbered into motion. He checked the brakes and engaged the nose wheel steering. Instinctively he looked to his left before turning. "Clear left."

Prairie Sentinel

THE WAHATOYA

"Clear right," the co-pilot responded. Pilots were paranoid about running into objects while still earth bound. They had the taxiway to themselves because it was a Saturday and there were no training flights scheduled. Ben stopped just short of the runway and the crew finished the Before Takeoff check list. Their headsets crackled.

"Tiger One-Eleven you're cleared for take-off. Winds are two-five-five at six knots. Altimeter setting is two-niner-eight-five. Contact Pueblo Tower on one-twenty-one point five after take-off."

The co-pilot responded, "Roger, altimeter two-niner-eight-five, cleared for take-off."

Ben rolled into take-off position and pressed his feet hard against the brakes as he advanced the throttles to full power. The engines roared and the B-24 strained against the brakes while Ben and his co-pilot scanned the engine instruments. Ben released the brakes and the plane began its take-off roll. When their speed had increased sufficiently Ben switched to the rudders for directional control, his boots dancing lightly on the pedals to keep the nose wheel on the runway centerline. He could feel the airplane's nose trying to lift off as they gathered speed. He held the nose down until he heard Bill call out, "Rotate." The airspeed indicator registered one-hundred fifteen knots when Ben eased the yoke back and the B-24 broke ground. Bill contacted Pueblo Tower and Ben began a right hand climbing turn and called for gear up.

Ben had been looking forward to this trip. It would be a nice break from flight instruction. He typically flew four training missions a day, teaching new B-24 pilots and their crews the finer points of operating the B-24. They practiced joining up in formation, simulated bombing runs and rehearsed various emergency procedures. Ben liked teaching the advanced maneuvers but it would be nice to fly a real mission, even a "milk run" like this, for a change of pace. He was looking forward to flying over the southern Colorado countryside. Even landing at a different airport would be a nice departure from routine.

Late yesterday his Squadron Commander had called him into his office. The Wing Commander of the newly formed 491st Bomb Group was also there. The Wing Commander almost never came into the squadron. Ben stood at attention.

"At ease, Ben. Please have a seat," Colonel Thomas, the Squadron Commander motioned to a chair. General Hayes asked, "How are the new arrivals doing, Ben?" Ben relaxed a little as he briefed the general about his students. He recounted a humorous story about a flight engineer from south Texas trying to communicate with his pilot who was raised in New Jersey.

Ben reenacted the conversation by exaggerating his own Texas drawl and then mimicking a New Jersey accent. They all had a good natured laugh.

Colonel Thomas spoke up. "Ben, we want you to put together a skeleton crew and fly down to Los Alamos tomorrow to pick up a VIP and fly him and a few other passengers back to Pueblo."

"Yes sir." Ben hesitated a moment. "Sir, I assume they know what to expect as to the lack of passenger comforts?"

"Don't worry about that. They know what not to expect."

So Ben had selected his crew. A typical (if there was such a thing) B-24 bombing mission required ten crew members. All Ben needed was a co-pilot and a flight engineer (sometimes called a crew chief) for such a short and simple trip. He had picked Bill Haley to be his co-pilot because he liked him and they shared a Texas heritage. Bill also happened to be an excellent pilot. Ben's selection of the flight engineer, Tony Franklin, was driven more by the young airman's performance on recent training flights and his obvious enthusiasm for his job. He was smarter than some of the young pilots and possessed an incredible ability to solve mechanical problems. Being selected for a special mission would be a definite feather in young Tony's cap and Ben wanted to recognize him for his performance.

The lumbering B-24 grudgingly gained airspeed after Bill retracted the landing gear and then the flaps. They settled into a comfortable climb at one-hundred fifty knots, increasing their altitude by eight hundred feet every minute or so. Ben enjoyed the feel of flying the empty aircraft. He had piloted many a take-off loaded down with eight-thousand pounds of bombs and over two-thousand pounds of fuel. An engine failure, during or right after take-off, on such a heavily loaded plane could have ended in a fiery catastrophe. Technically, the B-24 could fly with only two engines operating but the sudden loss of an outboard engine would create such an imbalance of torque, especially with all engines at full power, that the pilot probably could not control the plane. The combination of a loss of control, the low altitude and the heavy load of highly explosive materials made for an unimaginable scenario.

Ben had decided to level off at ten-thousand feet so they could enjoy the mountain scenery along the way. He climbed to ten-thousand five hundred feet, and eased back down to ten-thousand cruising altitude. This leveling-off technique, referred to as "getting on the step", allowed the aircraft to reach its cruising airspeed of one-hundred seventy knots with a minimum use of fuel. The B-24 had an autopilot but Ben chose to fly "hands on". Even though he spent hours of every day in a plane, he rarely got to fly himself and he didn't want to lose his touch. He made a few shallow turns back and forth either side of their invisible, southern aeronautical path. He enjoyed the feeling of directing such a powerful beast.

"Wow, look at that," exclaimed Bill. Towering above the horizon almost directly in front of them, were two magnificent mountain peaks crowned in radiant white. The morning sun sharpened the whiteness against the iridescent blue sky.

"Those are the Spanish Peaks." Ben chimed in after a minute. "The one on the right is called West Peak. It's thirteen-thousand six-hundred twenty-three feet high. The little brother, on the left, is East Peak and is "only" twelve-thousand seven-hundred eight feet high. Local legend says that the peaks were considered sacred by many of the Indian tribes who lived and hunted in the area. Supposedly, the Ute Indian tribe had quite a presence around those two mountains. One of their names for the two mountains was the Wahatoya which, at least by one interpretation, means "breasts of the earth".

Bill smiled but kept silent for a minute. "Well, there's quite a bit I could say about that but I'm going to restrain myself. The name certainly seems to fit."

The twin peaks seemed to fill their windshield as they flew closer. Ben kept correcting their course to provide plenty of clearance. The view of the peaks was magnificent as they came abreast of the titans. The young flight engineer, Tony, was spellbound by the sight of so much snow. Ben engaged the auto pilot so he could devote his attention to a few moments of scenic enjoyment.

Bill Haley dialed in the radio frequency their squadron commander had given them. Colonel Thomas had told them that due to the highly classified work being done at Los Alamos they would be landing at a remote strip. He had personally given them directions to call in on the frequency, which strangely, he had not written down. They were to call when they arrived over Albuquerque at an altitude of two-thousand feet.

"This is Tiger One-Eleven broadcasting in the blind" (he had been briefed rather emphatically to not repeat the frequency over the air). They waited.

"Tiger One-Eleven we read you five-by-five. Proceed south-west to a large, oval lake. The runway is about three miles due west of the lake. Call again when you have the runway in sight."

"Roger, Tiger One-Eleven." Bill looked at Ben. Ben just shrugged his shoulders. It was a very unusual approach; no tower, no traffic control, no weather report, and so far no runway. They flew over the lake and turned west. They should have seen the airport by now. Ben adjusted his seat, not really moving it, but the ritual was his signal to get in the approach/landing mode. He became more focused, his mind replaying all the procedures necessary to prepare the aircraft and himself for the landing. Still no runway.

"There it is, two o'clock." Bill pointed to the front and slightly right.

Ben banked right and saw an open pasture with a freshly mowed section approximating a make-shift runway. "What the . . ." Ben had gotten used to nice long, wide runways with center line stripes since he had returned from England. Landing in a field required a higher level of mental intensity and attention to detail. He flew over the pasture and down the length of the runway at an altitude of one-thousand feet. At the end of the runway he banked hard left and pulled the B-24 around in a tight turn. The g-forces pulled at their bodies. As Ben rolled out level after the hundred and eighty degree turn, Bill radioed, "Tiger One-Eleven is on left downwind."

"Tiger One-Eleven you're cleared to land."

"Before Landing Checklist," Ben called. He quickly verified his altitude and then looked to his left to confirm the plane's alignment and distance from the runway. When the end of the runway was roughly forty-five degrees to the left wing tip Ben started his left turn. He reduced the power almost to idle. Instead of flying a traditional box pattern with a distinct base leg, he was going to fly a continuous turn onto final approach.

"Landing gear down," he called. Bill lowered the landing gear handle and they felt the wheels disengage and thunk into landing position. Bill had already set the flaps to fifty percent. Ben compulsively verified that all the landing gear lights glowed green. "Flaps landing," Ben requested. Bill slid the flap handle all the way down and the flaps extended the rest of the way. Ben increased power slightly to maintain his approach airspeed. They were now in a very precarious position. There was a lot of drag (landing gear and flaps) hanging out, low airspeed, very low power settings and they were extremely close to the ground with the nose pointed down. Mistakes at this point could be deadly. Ben quickly and expertly scanned his instruments as the ground rushed up to meet their wheels. His mental checklist replayed automatically.

Gear down, airspeed good, flaps set, the nose tracking true and straight so there's no cross wind.

For the thousandth-plus time Ben's eyes and brain processed the image of the rising runway, the plane's attitude (relationship to the horizon) and speed and the sound of the engines. Ben eased the yoke back to begin his flare, searching for that perfect moment when the airplane stopped flying and the wheels kissed the runway. There was an old pilot saying, "A good

THE WAHATOYA

landing is one you walk away from." But every pilot that Ben knew always tried to grease their landings. When a pilot was especially proud of a smooth landing he would call the tower and ask them to confirm that his plane had touched down.

The touch-down and roll-out were uneventful. A nondescript vehicle with flashing lights met them and led them to a wide spot. Ben shut down the engines. The flight engineer had already opened the crew door. A man in a dark suit was waiting as Ben climbed out of the plane.

"Captain Curtis?"

"Yes, I'm Ben Curtis," Ben replied.

"Can I see your ID, please?" The man showed Ben his FBI badge.

Puzzled, Ben produced his military ID. The dark-suit examined it and returned it to him.

"You will be transporting five passengers back to Pueblo. You are not to speak to any of them. Do you understand?" The dark-suit never changed expression. His voice was flat, devoid of inflection or emotion. Ben felt a chill. He wasn't so sure he was having fun anymore.

Ploesti

"Yes, I understand." Ben had been yanked out of his casual, milk-run reverie when the dark suit began speaking. He flashed back to the last time he had had this feeling. It was shortly after the briefing for his last combat mission of World War Two. He and one-hundred seventy-seven other command pilots had been instructed to fly their B-24s, chock full of bombs, fuel and combat crews, one-thousand two hundred, low-level miles in an effort to bomb the living hell out of Germany's major refinery complex, Ploesti. The mission was code named Tidal Wave. Ben remembered ruefully that one of the enlisted crew members stood up after the briefing and asked the Colonel if the mission had been hatched by "some idiotic armchair warrior in Washington." This assessment was so close to the obvious truth that the Colonel didn't even chastise the young man. Nonetheless, they flew the mission.

The "armchair warrior" and others in Washington were sure that, due to the seclusion of the refinery complex, the Germans would not expect a raid and, consequently would not waste their defenses on such a remote target. Unfortunately for the five-hundred thirty-two crewmen who were killed, captured, interned or listed as missing in action as a result of the raid, the "armchair warriors" were dead wrong. Ben's plane was in the second wave and just when he thought things couldn't get any worse, they really went to hell. Two of the group commanders disagreed about the proper approach speed so B-24s arrived at different times. The lead navigator took a wrong turn. Adding insult to injury, clouds obscured much of the target area. Instead of pouncing on the target in one massive, coordinated surprise attack, most of the planes arrived in scattered bunches and were pounced on by waiting German fighters. The squandered opportunity and the staggering losses were exacerbated when intelligence sources, after the raid, reported that the output of the Ploesti complex had rebounded to an all time high.

Ben still had nightmares about that raid and the return flight. It was the only time he had lost a crew member. By the time he got over the target the sky was full of flak fired by antiaircraft cannons. German Me109s were swarming all over the sluggish B-24s, which were falling out of the sky right and left. Ben saw one plane practically disintegrate and watched in horror as one of the air crew bailed out only to have his chute catch on fire. Ben's navigator was yelling at him to correct the plane's course and the bombardier was screaming that he couldn't see the target through the cloud cover. Ben was praying. He knew his prayer was jumbled and incoherent. Could God make sense of what must have sounded like the equivalent of a spiritual machine gun?

Do I pray that our bombs kill only refinery workers and spare innocent civilians? Are the refinery workers also innocent or do they deserve death as much as German pilots? Ben's mind was racing. He struggled to keep focused on the tasks at hand. The problem was that he felt like he was losing track of the tasks.

They finally dropped their load of bombs. As Ben rolled the B-24 into a steep turn to escape that hell-on-high over the targets, the plane shuddered and almost rolled all the way over. Before Ben could react the windshield exploded and the cockpit was filled with fast moving shards of glass and shrapnel. He wrenched the yoke to counteract the aircraft's roll, but got no response. The plane's nose dropped and in the blink of an eye, the aircraft was in a deadly spin. The longer an airplane spins, the more violent becomes the spin. The aerodynamic forces, if unchecked, could tear the airplane apart long before it impacts the earth. Ben had seconds to act.

"Oh my God," Ben yelled. The g-forces had him pinned back in his seat. He could barely move his arms. He struggled with the yoke. His instincts took over. He could tell that the plane was spinning to the left. He rammed his right foot hard against the right rudder pedal and, even though it seemed counter intuitive, he pushed the nose over even farther. The plane's rotations slowed then stopped. He slowly began to apply back pressure to bring the plane out of its dive. Later he realized that the rapid loss of altitude caused by the spin may have saved them from the Me-109s as the German pilots could not have matched his rapid descent. All was not well though. An unfamiliar roar filled the cockpit.

Ben yelled into his microphone, "Somebody give me a damage report."

He was struggling to maintain control of the aircraft. His left hand was getting numb and blood was running into his eyes. It felt like a hurricane was blowing through the shattered windshield. Out of the corner of his eye he could see his co-pilot slumped over the plane's controls. The front of his flight suit was soaked in blood. Ben was all alone with the controls.

"Lieutenant Curtis, we lost part of the tail. We've got a bunch of holes in the fuselage. The waist gunner was blown away and we've got a bunch of cables blown apart."

Ben understood then why his rudders weren't responding. He finally had time to scan his engine instruments and saw that engine number four was out. He adjusted the trim and played with his throttle settings and cowl flap adjustments to compensate for the loss of rudder control. His crew confirmed that Airman and Waist Gunner Will Ford was missing and presumed dead. The gunner's position had taken a direct hit. A leaking fuel line required the crew to transfer fuel from one tank to another, which caused a momentary weight imbalance.

He wiped blood from his eyes. He was holding the yoke with his left arm wrapped around it. His right hand alternated between the yoke and the throttles. His quick action had stabilized the aircraft. Maybe all was not lost.

"Navigator, I can't see my altimeter or air speed indicator. What's our altitude and speed?" Ben yelled above the cockpit noise.

"We're barely maintaining seven-thousand feet. Our air speed is a hundred and fifty knots," Don Hagle,the navigator yelled into his left ear. "We're approximately fifty miles off course. Try to fly heading one-eight-five. That will get us back on course."

Ben nodded. "I need some help with the controls. Try to get Carl out of the co-pilot's seat and take his place."

Lt. Hagle wrestled the co-pilot out of his seat but needed help from one of the turret gunners to pull the limp body out of the cockpit. Amazingly the co-pilot was still breathing. The crew tore open first aid kits and stuffed all the bandages they could into his wounds to stop the bleeding. The navigator knew that he needed to stay at his station to monitor their progress and to keep them on track. He got the bombardier to sit in the co-pilot's seat to help Ben muscle the controls. It was taking all of Ben's quickly diminishing strength to hold the plane level. He was also constantly adjusting the throttles to maintain directional control. The rudders were worthless. None of the crew dared to think about how they were going to land.

But land they must.

Almost fourteen hours after taking off from the hell hole also known as Benghazi, Liberia, Lieutenant Ben Curtis lined up his crippled B-24 for an uncertain landing. He knew that they had lost massive amounts of hydraulic fluid so Ben decided to leave the landing gear retracted. If the gear got stuck halfway down because of the lack of hydraulic fluid, the impact of the landing would surely tear them off and probably cause even greater damage to the aircraft's belly after touch down. Ben needed to give the aircraft and the crew every possible chance to survive the high-risk landing. The leaking fuel lines

THE WAHATOYA   21

had soaked a portion of the plane's interior. Ben ordered the crew to secure themselves as best they could. He and the bombardier strapped themselves tightly into their seats. Ben was drifting in and out of consciousness. He was exhausted.

naiku

The scene at Benghazi was chaotic. Broken B-24s littered the runway. The ground crews couldn't move the debris quickly enough. Wounded crewmen were sprawled haphazardly among the wrecked airplanes. Ben pointed the aircraft's nose toward a sandy area paralleling the runway. He was out of time and he couldn't think clearly. The dying B-24 settled onto the blowing sands of Benghazi. Ben held the yoke as far back as he could for as long as he could. The hulking giant rattled across the hardscrabble kicking up a cloud of blinding sand. The aircraft's nose finally dropped to the ground and the aircraft slid around in a half turn before it ground to a halt.

Ben was barely conscious. Shrapnel had penetrated the cockpit, lodging in his left arm and in his forehead. The wounds caused a significant loss of blood and paralysis in his left hand. How he had managed to fly the airplane for five hours and keep his wits about him was beyond any of the doctors' imaginations. So after thirty-five combat missions, First Lieutenant Ben Curtis completed his final landing on foreign soil.

Congress awarded five Medals of Honor to pilots of the Ploesti raid, some posthumously. Lieutenant Curtis was awarded the Distinguished Flying Cross for "uncharacteristic bravery and determination to protect his crew, displaying heroic skill and loyalty." Ben was surprised. Actually he was in awe when notified that he would be honored. He insisted that he only did what any pilot would have done to survive. He didn't fully appreciate the magnitude of his actions that day until he began receiving letters from the parents of his surviving crew members. Airman and Nose Gunner Randy Wilshire's father wrote, "When so many brave young men have lost their lives in the service of their country, we struggled with an unreasonable guilt that Randy had survived and would soon return home. But the more we learned about the inordinate skill and bravery required to bring your terribly damaged plane and crew home, the more we realized that Randy's survival was no fluke of war. It was an act of God manifested in your strength and resolve and it helped us celebrate Randy's life instead of dwelling on the tragic loss of so many others. We can never thank you enough."

The letter from Will Ford's father, though, was the most memorable.

"Dear Lieutenant Curtis," it began. "Thank you for your thoughtful letter about Will and how he conducted himself as a crew member. As you can imagine we are terribly distraught over the death of our only son. Our days are empty and our grief is almost unbearable. We have taken a great deal of comfort from the letters, including yours, from his friends and fellow crew members. Every one of the surviving crew has written us or visited us. Those letters and personal visits have revealed to us your uncompromising dedication and devotion to your crew. Knowing how hard you fought to save your crew is somehow comforting to us because we know that Will was beyond saving. We no longer ask ourselves the nagging question, *was there anything else that could have been done to save him?* We now know that he was in God's hands that day."

Ben wept after reading that letter. Until then Will's death had been abstract because they didn't have to carry his body off the plane after crash landing. He had just disappeared. For the first time he understood the scale of his efforts to save his crew that day.

"Captain Curtis, are you okay?"

Letters

The Wahatoya

The swirling dust devils of Benghazi faded away to the soft April breeze of New Mexico. Ben could feel the sweat on his forehead. That flight from Ploesti had never really ended. Ben knew that he needed to work on that; maybe after the war.

"Oh, yeah, sorry. I got distracted," Ben replied to his co-pilot.

They both watched as four more black-suits exited a van that had pulled up next to their plane. Two of them were helping yet another man who seemed to be having trouble getting out. Then they saw why. His hands were bound with a long chain that extended around his waist. His hands were in front and the chain extended to his feet, which were similarly shackled.

"Holy cow," Bill exhaled.

"My sentiments exactly," Ben responded.

The B-24 had not been designed for ease-of-entry and it was almost comical to watch the FBI agents struggle to hoist and pull their—what? prisoner, companion, passenger into the plane's belly. None of them laughed though and they did not offer their assistance. The black-suit-in-charge watched impassively. He then turned to Ben and told him, "We need to leave as soon as possible, Captain Curtis."

Ben nodded. The three crew members walked to the plane. Ben and Bill Haley completed their walk-around inspection and then pulled themselves up through the bomb bay door to the flight deck. Tony, the flight engineer, started up the internal APU (auxiliary power unit) and plugged in his headset so he could communicate with the pilot while monitoring the start of the engines from the ground. After he was on board, Tony checked on the passengers and made sure they were secured for take-off. He then joined the pilot and co-pilot on the flight deck.

"Captain, they've got that guy shackled to the floor. What the hell do you think is going on?"

"I have no idea, Tony. I'll just be glad to get us home."

THE WAHATOYA   25

The take-off was uneventful. Ben requested that the radio voice (Ben had no idea where he was located) inform Pueblo Tower that they were airborne and that their ETA (estimated time of arrival) at Pueblo was fifteen-thirty (three thirty in the afternoon). When Ben leveled off at ten-thousand feet they were flying in and out of the clouds. He continued on up to twelve-thousand feet in search of clear skies. The weather man in Pueblo had assured him that they could expect clear weather all the way to Los Alamos and back. When they were still in the clouds at twelve-thousand feet Ben began to worry. They had been airborne for forty-five minutes and would soon be approaching the peaks of the Wahatoya. The clouds were getting darker by the minute. Ben decided to climb well above the top of West Peak, the higher of the two mountains, so they would clear it with plenty of room to spare. He leveled off at fifteen-thousand feet. The turbulence was getting worse by the minute.

"Captain Curtis, we're losing altitude." Bill reported.

Ben had been so intent on keeping the wings level while flying through the turbulence that he had engaged the altitude-hold mode of the autopilot. The turbulence must have caused it to exceed its tolerances, which triggered the autopilot's disengagement. Ben's altimeter showed an altitude of fourteen thousand feet. He increased power and raised the airplane's nose to regain altitude.

"Damn it. Where's my power?"

Bill checked his instruments. "Ben, we're losing airspeed!" His alarm filled the cockpit. Ben looked out the left window. He could see a whitish shadow that hugged the leading edge of the left wing. A deadly film of ice was growing on both wings. Ben knew that the propellers were probably icing up also. A combination of very moist air and the cold temperatures at high altitude could cause ice to form on wings and propellers. As the ice built up on the aircraft's surfaces it not only added weight at an alarming rate, it disrupted the airflow over and above the wings. This disruption robbed the wings of their lift. No lift—no flight. The sudden and unexpected turn of weather had caught both Ben and Bill off guard. They had not even considered turning on the plane's anti-icing equipment. That system, which directed heat to the wings' leading edges, was effective for preventing ice build up but was not very good at removing it. Ben could take them to a lower altitude where the air was warmer but he knew they were in the vicinity of two mountains. There was one other maneuver he could try. If he could put some g-forces on the wings, they just might flex enough to cause the ice to crack and fall away. He pushed the yoke forward and sent the plane into a deliberate descent. He then pulled the yoke back suddenly to stop the descent. He was hoping that these abrupt maneuvers would stress the wings enough to crack the ice. Ben also knew that the extra weight of the ice made the wings more susceptible to structural failure during extreme maneuvers. Ben could feel no difference in the sluggish controls. Their airspeed was still slowing. They were losing the battle to stay airborne.

"What the hell is going on up here?" The black-suit-in-charge yelled into the cockpit. He was holding on to the sides of the cockpit door for dear life and his face was deadly pale.

Ben's mind was racing. Their only hope was to descend to a lower altitude where warmer air could dissipate the ice, or at least lessen its deadly hold on their airplane. Worst case . . . it would be better to set the plane down on a highway or in a field under control than to stay up here until the plane fell out of the sky.

"Tony, help the passengers get ready for a crash landing," he yelled. "Bill, broadcast on guard channel (emergency frequency) our location and that we're going to try for an emergency landing."

Bill changed frequencies and began a rapid-fire transmission. He repeated it four or five times without pausing. He stopped to listen for acknowledgement. Then he looked down at the console to verify that he had selected the proper frequency.

"Oh dear God," Ben exclaimed loudly.

Bill jerked his head up. A vein of bright sunlight had broken through the gloom and was reflecting off the whitest immoveable cloud he had ever seen.

naiku

Ben banked hard to the right and jammed his throttles all the way open. He avoided a head-on collision but the right wing slammed into the mountain face and broke apart. The plane's belly contacted the mountain and slid down a long snow field. The left wing swung around hard, dragging its propellers across the icy ground. The steel blades crumpled like tinfoil. The bodies in the belly of the fuselage flew around like rag dolls. The force of the collision ripped the tail section apart and snow poured in, filling the rear of the plane's interior. The snow probably snuffed out any sparks before they could ignite the spilled fuel. The cockpit was peeled open and the co-pilot's seat was gone, probably expelled by the explosive force of the initial crash. The battered B-24 came to a jarring stop as it careened into a stand of giant fir trees. Silence enveloped the broken hulk.

Wreckage

naiku

Ben reluctantly regained consciousness. Oblivion was so quiet and peaceful . . . and pain free. He was confused. His B-24 had been shot to hell over Peloesti but he had nursed it back to Benghazi with his crew's help and sheer force of will. The old girl had settled onto that improvised sand runway kind of hard, but with much less mayhem than he had expected.

What the hell happened? Since when did it snow in the desert? Where were the medics? He had injured crewmembers, damn it! Medic! Medic!

His own shouts jolted him awake to an icy hell of carnage and death and desolation.

Missing

"What do you mean, they're overdue?" General Hayes shouted into the phone. He listened for a minute. "I'll be right there. Make sure Colonel Thomas is there too." Twenty minutes later, General Hayes erupted into the conference room of the Command Center. Emergencies and crises were no stranger to Roger Hayes. He had earned his stars by managing and maneuvering through life-and-death cataclysms from Pearl Harbor to Manila. But Pueblo, Colorado? This was supposed to be his version of a milk run before he retired—sort of like easing out quietly. *Oh well.*

"Be seated, gentlemen. What's the status of Ben Curtis's flight?"

"Sir, we received a radio transmission at twelve hundred hours from an unidentified source reporting that Captain Curtis had just taken off and was estimating arrival at Pueblo at fifteen-thirty hours." Major Bradshaw was the Officer of the Day in the Flight Operations Command Post. All eyes looked at the large clock on the wall as if maybe by some miracle they had all misinterpreted the current hour. But it was unmistakable. The B-24 and its crew were forty-five minutes overdue.

Tech Sergeant Hanks stood up next. "General, when Captain Curtis received his weather briefing this morning the National Weather Service was forecasting clear skies for the next forty-eight hours. I matched their data to our own readings and concurred with their prediction. Since then, we've seen a low weather system begin to form over the Gulf of Mexico. The jet stream has unexpectedly shifted south and is pulling large amounts of moisture from the Gulf. That low pressure system is bumping up against the high that was supposed to be keeping our skies clear. We tried to call Los Alamos to give Captain Curtis a weather advisory but no one would acknowledge that he was even there."

"Thank you Sergeant." General Hayes had complete faith in his weather staff. They were some of the best. He cursed under his breath. *Damn secrets.* He had seen it happen many times before. When operations were shrouded in secrecy it never failed that the one person who needed to know the secret didn't, and that omission often cost lives. *Damn. Damn. Damn.* Now he had to call the last person in the world he wanted to talk to.

"Excuse me, General." The First Sergeant burst into the room. "We just got a call from the Huerfano County Sheriff. One of his deputies took a report of a low flying aircraft near La Veta about thirteen hundred. A rancher had gone outside to check on his horses when he heard an airplane fly over. He said that the engine noise was variable—loud then quieter. He couldn't see the plane because of the overcast but he was sure of the noise."

"Thank you, Sergeant Moody." General Hayes stood up. "Get our emergency response team activated and get them to that Sheriff's office as soon as possible," he directed Major Bradshaw. "Keep me informed, gentlemen, that's all for now." The men came to attention as the general left the room.

General Hayes dialed another number. This one connected him to an office in Washington, D.C. "Michael? This is Roger Hayes. We have a big problem." The general outlined the events of the day. His good friend at the other end listened without comment.

"I'll have to brief the President about this," Michael told him. "We'll send a team to Pueblo. This could get real messy, Roger."

Roger Hayes replaced the phone. "What the hell is going on?" That was also the question two days earlier when Michael Morrison had called him and outlined the mission to send a B-24 to Los Alamos to pick up a "special" passenger who would be accompanied by FBI agents. Upon arriving at Pueblo Army Air Field the FBI agents would transport the passenger to the federal prison at Canon City, Colorado, only thirty miles from Pueblo. Michael would not tell him any more about the passenger. Obviously, he was very important to the U.S. government. Roger Hayes allowed himself a moment to reflect on his friendship with "Mikey", his college roommate and friend.

naiku

They had both aspired to political careers. Roger Hayes had been seduced by flying and becoming a pilot instead, and had never looked back. He was a natural leader, and had advanced rapidly in the military. He had earned his first star after Pearl Harbor. He and Michael had not spoken much since the war began but Roger knew that he was in some hush-hush job at the Pentagon. Then, out of the blue, Michael had called with the request for a special flight. Roger couldn't help being just a little perturbed at his friend's role in all of this. The "special mission" had put his best pilot and a crew in danger. He was going to raise holy hell if this turned out to be some dumb-ass Washington boondoggle.

naiku

Sheriff Lonnie Dunn brushed the snow from his jacket. He had learned to expect the unexpected from the weather this time of year. He walked into his office and was greeted by five very serious looking strangers.

"Holy shit, it looks like a salesman's convention in here," he exclaimed. He looked at his deputy, who shrugged and shook his head. The three FBI agents stepped forward first and presented their badges and credentials and introduced themselves. Michael stepped forward with his. The sheriff looked at it for a minute. Michael's was signed by the President of the United States.

"Well, okay, you've got the biggest dick in the room, that's for sure," the sheriff smiled.

Roger Hayes turned his head quickly to hide his smile. He liked this sheriff. He knew how to cut right through the pomp and ceremony. Roger made a mental note that this guy probably got things done. He extended his hand to the sheriff and introduced himself. He and Michael had agreed that Roger would sign out on leave and wear civilian clothes so his uniform and rank wouldn't attract attention.

"I'm just along for the ride."

"Yeah, I'll bet you are," smiled the sheriff.

Michael had flown in on a military plane the day before with the FBI agents. After the two old friends had said their hellos, Roger Hayes took Michael into his office.

"What's going on Michael? I'm missing a crew and an airplane and I'm about to get really pissed off at Washington."

Michael looked directly in his eyes and told him, "I don't doubt you are, Roger. That's why I came along, to explain everything to you in person. By the way, some of what I'm going to tell you—I could be shot for disclosing. But I trust you with my life and I understand how you feel about your crew. How much do you know about the Manhattan Project?" Roger thought for a minute. "Pretty much what the other generals know. There's supposedly a secret project to develop a weapon that could conceivably end the war. Wait a minute—that project is supposedly at Los Alamos."

Michael was nodding. "We are getting very close to testing the first prototype of an atomic bomb. Roger, it is more destructive than any of us ever imagined and it will transform the United States into the most powerful

Willie's Night Out

country on earth overnight. The Russians and the Germans are working on their own versions of a weapon. We think the Germans are closest but we don't know exactly how close they are to testing it. Our immediate problem is that our intelligence service uncovered good evidence that one of the scientists who has been working on the Manhattan Project was getting ready to defect to Germany with a critical formula. Depending on how far along they are, this formula could allow them to jump ahead of us and develop the bomb first. They could decimate London. Ben Curtis's passenger is that scientist. The FBI was going to take him to the prison at Canon City and question him until they found out what he was about to divulge. Even if they couldn't break him, they were going to keep him there until after the war for sure. We have got to find out if he survived that crash and if he did we have to get him off that mountain."

"What about my crew?"

"That's why I wanted you along, to be on hand when and if we have to make decisions that involve your crew. I've got to tell you though, the number one objective here is to capture the defector or recover his body. My orders come directly from the President."

Roger understood the chain of command all too well and he understood that his friend Michael, a civilian, outranked him in this matter.

"In all likelihood any survivors will be together so I can't imagine that we're going to have to haggle over priorities," Roger offered.

"I agree. Our biggest problem will be getting someone up that mountain."

They huddled around a large map that the sheriff had pulled out.

"Right here is where the rancher heard the engine sounds," the sheriff pointed on the map. It was clear that the plane had been on a collision course with West Peak. They had not received any reports of a plane crashing, and had no radio contact with the crew since then, so they agreed that their first search efforts should be directed toward West Peak.

"There's an old mining road, a trail really, that begins about here and would be a logical start for a search team." The sheriff was shaking his head. "Gentlemen, it will be almost impossible for a search team to get up that mountain through all that snow."

Roger glanced at Michael. Michael responded, "Sheriff, all I can tell you is that it is a matter of national security that we find that crew and their passengers. We need your help." The sheriff nodded slowly then spoke. "The first thing we need is somebody who knows that mountain, and isn't afraid of a little snow. I need a few hours. Why don't we meet back here first thing in the morning?"

The sheriff called the LaVeta Inn and got rooms for the visitors. They were anxious to start the search but they all knew that to start out without proper planning and the right people could be a disaster for the search team as well as for the crew and passengers. At least the snow had stopped so Roger allowed himself a glimmer of hope that they would find his crew alive.

Sheriff Dunn decided that driving would take too long because the roads would be next to impossible with all the fresh snow. He saddled up his best snow horse, Willie, and started out in the dark. Willie snorted and shook his head vigorously as if to protest the late hour. "Yeah, I know. This is a bitch of a time to take a trip but it can't be helped." The sheriff knew there was only one man who could find that airplane and its crew.

Sven Curry

"Hello, Sven. I need your help." Sven Curry greeted the sheriff as he greeted all visitors, day or night. He turned his back and walked back in his cabin. Most folks would have been insulted and might have thought Sven didn't want to talk to them but Sheriff Dunn simply followed Sven into his small rock house. It had taken the sheriff several years to figure out Sven's ways. He was a man of few words and even fewer social graces. He rarely asked for help himself but was always available when others needed a helping hand. No one knew for sure how old Sven was but the old-timers calculated he was nearing eighty.

Sven's parents had arrived from Sweden with his older brother and sister when he was three weeks old. The two or three really old timers remembered him as a child. Sven never talked about his childhood, even to Sheriff Dunn, who had become one of his few friends over the years. But old man Bowman had once told the sheriff about the day that Sven's father was killed by a young Ute Indian as the result of a horrible mis-understanding. It seems that Sven's older sister Becky had wandered away from the house while looking after her younger brother, Jahn. Two young Ute hunters had wounded a buck and were pursuing the dying animal through thick brush. The buck and one of the braves crashed out of the brush near where Becky was standing. Startled, she began screaming. Her father heard the screams and ran to her, his rifle in his hands. What he saw next was an Indian holding a bow and his daughter screaming her head off. He shot the young brave just as the Ute's hunting companion broke out of the brush in pursuit of the wounded deer. The second Ute watched his friend die and saw a white man pointing a rifle at him. He killed Sven's father thinking that he was about to shoot him too. Jahn, Sven's older brother, saw it all. He ran and hid in the surrounding woods for several days. He was never the same again.

Becky recovered and helped her mother take care of the two boys. When Sven was about ten years old his sister married a young Swede fellow from a neighboring family. Sven's mother, who had never recovered from that horrible day, couldn't cope with the loneliness and with trying to raise two sons on her own. She packed up the boys and headed back to Sweden with a group of other Swedish families who likewise had found the Cuchara valley too demanding and inhospitable. On the second day of their exodus, Sven slipped out of the wagon and headed back to the only home he had ever known. He hadn't planned to strike out on his own and hadn't thought about how he would survive. He just knew he couldn't leave. Sven had become quite self sufficient out of necessity. There was some food left in their recently abandoned home and Sven carefully rationed it out over the first few days he was back. Growing up without a father, he had not learned to hunt as most boys his age. He didn't even have a gun. After three days without food (except for some bitter-tasting roots he had pulled from the river bank), and driven by a growing desperation, Sven sought out some form of human contact.

Old Sai'-ar knew she was being watched while she gutted and cleaned her catch-of-the-day. The young white boy was not very successful at hiding but he was keeping a respectful distance. Sai'-ar couldn't have done him harm even if she had wanted to. It was difficult enough for her to bend over and recover the trapped fish. She wrapped the fish in her leather pouch and very deliberately placed her cleaning knife in another pouch hanging from her waist band.

"Boy, come out and show your self," she spoke without looking directly at Sven. Sven, who thought he was being very stealthy, hesitated a minute then summoned all his courage and stood up. He half expected a swarm of Indian braves to swoop down and scalp him, but he was too hungry to care. Sai'-ar gathered an armful of firewood and gave it to Sven to carry for her.

"Try to be useful." He hugged his new burden tightly. It somehow restored his dignity, and lessened the shame of having to ask for food.

He strode into the Ute camp feeling like a helper rather than a supplicant. Sai'-ar presented him to the curious tribe members as "this scrawny little white boy who offered to help an old lady with her burden, even though all she had to offer in return was breakfast." The adults just shook their heads at Sai'-ar dragging yet another wayward orphan into their camp to feed. The children soon formed a jostling, giggling ring around Sven, watching him eat. They were always mesmerized by white children.

Sven became a fixture in the Ute camp. If Sai'-ar didn't have chores for him he hustled around the camp looking for work to do. He had been without a motherly influence ever since his father had died. His mother had barely been able to function as provider to her three children, much less nurture them

Sven, the Helper

after her husband was killed. Sai'-ar's grandmotherly attention, though harsh at times, rushed in and filled the emptiness in the young boy's soul. When Towaoc, the Ute's chief, expressed his concern about the white boy becoming a permanent fixture in the camp, Sai'-ar sharply reminded him of how he, Towaoc, the Great Chief, as a young boy had been plucked from certain death by the kindly Spanish priest, Father Miguel. The priest had become a surrogate father to the young Apache and in loving concert with Sai'-ar had raised him to become a great Ute chief. Towaoc grudgingly acknowledged that she was right and gave up.

Rescued

During warm weather Sven sometimes traveled to his family's house and slept there. He had slowly begun to talk about his family and how he came to be alone. Towaoc eventually learned of the young orphan's part in one of their tribe's most painful and deadly incidents. The accidental killing of a Ute brave and of Sven's father had triggered a bloody battle between the Utes and the Spanish settlers and had caused a turning point in their relationship. Years later, when Towaoc was nearing death, he talked to Sven about his father's death. He wanted Sven to understand that the killings were the result of a terrible misunderstanding between the Ute braves and his father. Towaoc wanted him to know that he was sorry for Sven's loss.

After Towaoc became an old man and had grown to trust Sven, he had shown Sven the cave hidden behind Chaparral Falls. He showed Sven a stack of leather satchels full of Spanish gold coins. He told Sven how the coins came into his possession as a result of another bloody incident with the Spanish. The coins were a curse for his tribe and had caused the deaths of many of their young braves. Perhaps Sven would find an honorable use for them someday.

naiku

It was during one of Sven's trips back to his house that he found a new friend. He had stopped to drink from the Cuchara River and was down on his knees cupping the cold water with his hands. He heard a small, shrill whimper coming from behind a thorny brush not far from the water. He never would have heard it if he hadn't been kneeling down, and even then it was barely audible over the noise of the rushing water. Sven cocked his head and focused on the tiny noise. He quietly crawled on his hands and knees in the direction of the mournful sound. There it was again—something between a baby's cry and a kitten's mew. His face was close to the ground to avoid the thorny branches and he was almost on top of the noise by the time he spotted the source. It was a tiny wolf pup, alone in the remaining battlefield of what had been a vicious and bloody confrontation. The pup's mother had been terribly mauled. Parts of her body had been scattered about, some of it dragged away through the brush. Sven saw the tracks. A mountain lion had invaded the mama wolf's den and killed her pups, except this one. Who knows how it survived. It appeared to be about four or five weeks old. Its fur was matted with blood but there were no visible wounds. Sven reached out to it and was immediately bitten on the finger by a row of tiny, sharp teeth. He jerked his hand back and laughed.

"You're a feisty little devil, aren't you?" He was more careful the next time and used his left hand to draw the comically snarling pup's attention while he reached his right hand around behind it and grabbed it by the nape of its neck. Sven's grip was firm enough to immobilize the pup without hurting it but when he picked the pup off the ground, it yelped in pain. Sven could see that its right front leg was broken. He gathered the pitiful little wad of fur into his arms and pressed him against his chest so it could feel Sven's heart beating. The pup nestled into his arm and quieted. Sven walked through the shadows of the evening to Father Miguel, whom every one knew could never turn down a cry for help, whether from a broken little boy or an orphaned wolf pup.

Sven was right. Miguel rounded up fresh goat's milk and mixed in some cornmeal. He soaked a rag in the gooey mess and had Sven force a corner of it in the pup's mouth. After a minute of struggle, he got a taste of the slimy mixture and began chewing and sucking with gusto. While the pup was distracted, Miguel made a tiny splint for the broken leg and wrapped it gently. The exhausted pup fell asleep with the makeshift nipple still in its mouth, which continued to work. Sven cleaned its grimy, matted fur and determined that their little friend was a male.

"You should stay here tonight. He'll need to be fed often during the night," Father Miguel told him.

Sven curled up on a sleeping mat and crooked his arm so that the pup was sleeping against his body. Miguel watched Sven care for his newfound friend and thought to himself, *there's no better medicine for the soul, than taking care of somebody else.*

After about a week of convalescence, the pup began walking and playing. The crude splint caused an awkward limp. Miguel had redone the splint so that the pup could put weight on it and hobble around. He looked like a tiny drunk and fell down often until he learned how to use his pegleg. Sven

The Orphan

played with him constantly and began feeding him scraps of meat. The little guy was always ravenous and gulped down the tidbits without even chewing. Sven decided that he needed to go home. He was getting restless.

"What should I name him, Father?"

"He deserves a strong name because he survived and he will need to be strong for the rest of his life. Lobo means wolf in Spanish. With such a name he will never forget who he is." Father Miguel had a twinkle in his eye.

"Lobo it is," Sven replied as he swept Lobo up in his arms. "Thank you, Father, for all your help."

Father Miguel hugged Sven and rubbed Lobo's head.

Sven became totally absorbed in nursing Lobo back to health. The leg healed and Lobo continued to grow. His coat thickened and turned a shiny black. He and Sven caused quite a stir the first time they walked into the Ute camp together. The Utes did not keep pets as a rule. There were a few scraggly mutts who hung around the camp. They lived on scraps and played with the smaller children. When Lobo strode into camp, the mutts cowered and slunk out of sight. The braves gathered around to admire Lobo but he largely ignored them. He barely tolerated humans other than Sven. Some of the Indians in the camp believed that Sven must have special powers to be able to walk with the wolf. Others were afraid to have such an animal in the camp. He convinced them that Lobo would help protect them from wild animals. Sven would play with Lobo to show the wolf's playful side. They became inseparable, two abandoned creatures who found refuge in each other.

Survival

Ben opened his eyes. *Dear God, it's not fair.* He looked around. His co-pilot was obviously dead. Ben unsnapped his own shoulder harness and tried to pull himself forward. His feet were numb from the cold but everything else seemed to be functioning. He noticed that the front of his flight suit was soaked with blood. He ran his hand over his face and then through his hair. His hand came away bloody. Fortunately for him the cold temperature had slowed the loss of blood and probably saved his life. It was a nasty gash that had opened his scalp from front to back almost directly down the middle of his head. He stumbled out of the seat and grabbed a bracket on the overhead panel to steady himself. The destruction was devastating. He climbed over debris and twisted metal and made his way toward the cabin. The door from the cockpit to the cabin had been torn off its hinges. Ben's feet began to tingle as his circulation improved from moving around. His finger tips were hurting from the frigid temperature even though he still had his flight gloves on. He lowered himself into the cabin, dreading what he might see. Two of the FBI agents were crammed into a corner partially covered by twisted metal. Ben picked his way to the bodies and tried to find a pulse or other signs of life. Nothing. There should be three more agents. Suddenly Ben felt movement. A piece of wreckage had moved against his boot. He carefully began removing debris and metal fragments.

"Please help me." A raspy voice cried out.

"Hang on. I'm working as fast as I can." Ben removed a bundle of frayed cables. There! It was the man chained to the floor. Ben realized that the prisoner was wearing only a lightweight coat. At least Ben had his flight jacket. But none of them had anticipated being stranded in the mountains. Ben quickly checked the man for injuries. The chained leg looked broken. First things first. He went to the survival bag and pulled out all of the cold weather gear, which included heavy duty fur-lined parkas. He replaced his own flight jacket and wrestled one of the parkas onto the injured passenger/prisoner. Ben then rummaged through the pockets of the dead agents. One of them had a key ring that held handcuff-type keys. He unlocked the prisoner's hands first and then the feet. Ben wrestled with the thought that maybe he should leave the man shackled since the FBI had locked him up. *Like he's going anywhere with a broken leg, snowed in on the top of a mountain.* That thought ended very quickly.

I've got to start a fire, or we're both going to freeze to death. Right, inside an airplane, with fuel all around. But the fuel tanks are in the wings and if the wings had broken apart the fuel would have spilled outside. True, there were fuel lines that connected the tanks but he couldn't smell any fumes. Ben looked at the overhead wiring and metal piping in an effort to spot any dripping fuel or wet spots. He decided that it was worth the risk. He cleared a place on the aircraft's metal floor and built a fire pit out of torn metal parts. Then he piled up padding and webbing to burn. There was plenty of ventilation through the wreckage to avoid asphyxiation. Ben found matches in the survival kit. He winced as he struck the first match, anticipating a loud boom and a bright flash. Evidently he had been right and there were no fumes to ignite. The fire struggled and Ben had to nurse it to life with small bits of paper. He would need wood for a sustainable fire.

The prisoner (it occurred to Ben that they were both prisoners) groaned in pain and looked at Ben for the first time. "What happened?" he whispered.

"We crashed into a mountain. We're the only survivors and I think you have a broken leg." The man winced in pain when he tried to flex that leg. "How long have we been here?"

"About two or three hours, I'm guessing. I really need to stabilize that leg. Are you up to it?" The man started breathing heavily. "I . . . I . . . don't know. Give me a minute."

"What's your name," Ben asked.

"Daniel Frost," he replied.

"Well, I'm Ben Curtis. I'm the pilot. I was the pilot, that is."

Daniel smiled weakly. "Did you unlock me?"

"Yes, I did. I don't think you're going anywhere."

Ben, like all Army Air Force pilots, had received basic first aid training, which included first responder training. If he didn't stabilize the broken bone there was a risk that the broken ends would sever an artery. It wouldn't be pretty but combat life-saving techniques seldom were. He located two straight metal parts and cut two lengths of thick webbing.

"This is going to hurt like hell, Daniel."

THE WAHATOYA   45

Daniel began hyper-ventilating and grabbed two metal supports. Ben's forehead was sweating. He positioned his hands above and below where he was pretty sure the break had occurred. Daniel screamed and his body convulsed in pain. Ben worked quickly and tried to align the broken bone. He then placed the metal splints on each side of Daniel's leg and secured them in place with webbing at the top and the bottom.

Daniel was sobbing, "Oh God, that hurts. It hurts."

Ben was soaked in sweat. Listening to someone in pain was bad enough, but to be the one causing that pain was much worse. Ben searched the First Aid kit, looking for anything that might alleviate Daniel's agony. He found an ampule of morphine, which he used to inject Daniel. It took about fifteen minutes to take effect and Daniel's breathing slowly returned to normal. Ben just hoped that he hadn't made the injury worse.

After Ben had calmed down he started to look for a way out of the plane. It was a bomber, not a passenger plane so it didn't have doors in the side of the fuselage. The crew always entered the plane through the bomb bay door in the bottom of the fuselage. Ben climbed over the tangle of metal toward the tail and discovered that the left vertical stabilizer had broken apart, leaving a gaping hole. It was here that he found the bodies of the other FBI agents. *All present and accounted for.* Desperation gripped Ben's heart. He didn't know if he could do this alone.

He stuck his head out and, for the first time, saw the crash site. He could see the initial impact site and a long, wide swath in the snow where the wreckage had slid. They were jammed up against several large trees, which had interrupted their journey down the mountain. Ben climbed out onto the steep terrain and sank to his knees in snow. He had to hold onto the wreckage to keep from sliding down the mountain. He walked around to the part of the mountain above the plane and began picking up broken pieces of branches knocked down by the force of the impact. He also scooped up snow to carry inside and melt into drinking water.

How long is it going to take them to find us? He wondered.

Roger and Michael, along with the FBI agents, had just seated themselves at the Bright and Early Café in La Veta. Sheriff Dunn and Sven Curry followed close behind. The FBI agents and Michael and Roger were momentarily taken aback. Sven was a rangy six feet tall or so and looked trim even in his winter attire. He walked with a stride that spoke of efficiency and purpose. Roger thought that he had the no-nonsense bearing of a general. Michael was taken with Sven's intense gaze, anchored by his blue eyes. No one else in the café had taken notice of Sven's arrival, but the group of strangers was transfixed by the sight of his hair. It hung almost to his shoulders and was gathered into a ponytail. None of them had ever seen a man wearing a ponytail.

"Good morning, gentlemen." Sheriff Dunn looked tired. "Please introduce yourselves to Sven Curry. He's going to lead the search and rescue team." Michael took the lead and stood up. He introduced himself and his companions. He didn't offer his hand to Sven. Correctly, he had sensed that Sven didn't like to waste time or effort on social niceties. Michael and Sven locked eyes for a brief moment, each taking measure of the other.

He's a hard man, thought Michael. *That's alright. We need a hard man for this job.* Michael had worked for hard men. He had commanded hard men. He had even killed hard men in the line of duty. Sven revealed nothing of his silent assessment of Michael. Sven knew that time would tell. The mountain would test all of them before they were done.

The sheriff pulled over an empty table. While everyone ordered breakfast, he unrolled a map across the top of the work space.

"Sven and I agree that the plane more than likely crashed on this side of West Peak. I'm basing this mainly on where Rob Johnson was when he heard the sound of the engines and the direction he says the sound was moving." He pointed to the map and moved his pencil/pointer as if drawing the plane's flight path. "Of course the mountain and the clouds can play tricks on a man's hearing, but it seems the most likely place to start looking. What do you boys think?"

Michael asked, "Is there any type of shelter they could possibly be using?"

Sheriff Dunn shook his head. "There's an abandoned silver mine about here. The entrance to the Bulls Eye mine is mostly filled in. I haven't been up there in years but it's possible that they could move enough rocks out to provide some shelter from the falling snow and from the wind. But I doubt they would even see it though given all the fresh snow."

"What are the distances and time we're talking about here?" Michael looked at Sven, who had stayed silent so far.

"I can reach the summit here," he pointed, "in about four hours if I'm by myself. If I have to wait on others, it'll take an extra two hours. We need to get started so we can get most of the climbing done before dark. That way we can be near the summit at first light, and start looking for signs of the crash. There may be slide marks if the wind and snow haven't covered them. That would point us in the right direction."

THE WAHATOYA   47

Michael considered for a minute. He wanted to be the first one to reach the defector, but he had been out of the field for too long. His last field operation had been over six months ago and he could not afford to slow the search and rescue down. His stint as intelligence liaison between the President, the military branches and the FBI had dulled his physical conditioning and combat reflexes. He would have to rely on the agents.

"I would like to send two of these agents with you. They're very experienced outdoorsmen. They both have participated in numerous rescue missions and they have extensive wilderness medical training." Sven was not impressed. He wanted to inspect their cold weather gear. After rejecting most of what the FBI had sent and replacing it with gear from the sheriff's office and the local hardware store, Sven was ready to go. The roads were clear enough for the caravan to travel by truck and horse trailer to the base of the Wahatoya. They would start up West Peak on horseback.

naiku

Back at the sheriff's office Michael looked at the map and asked Sheriff Dunn how they could possibly travel up the mountain on horseback with that much snow on the ground. "Well, that's one of Sven's little secrets. There's a canyon that starts right about here. He showed me the entrance once but it's so well hidden that I probably couldn't find it again. Most people don't know about it. The Utes used it as a secret trail to get in and out of their camps without being seen by the Spanish settlers. According to Sven, the topography of the mountain and the angle of the canyon walls work together to keep the canyon floor clear of snow almost all year long. I guess the winds figure in that puzzle somehow too. He claims that he can go almost to the summit of West Peak on horseback."

"You see, Sven grew up with the Ute tribe that made their spring and summer camp around here. He told me that they called it the "Canyon of Tears" because that was the canyon where a band of rogue Spanish traders massacred ten or twelve of the tribe's young warriors, teenagers really. The Spaniards had hired the young braves to help them unload some pack horses. When they were done they killed all the braves to hide their secret. The Spaniards had stolen a boat load of gold coins from a Spanish wagon train transporting gold to the new country. The braves had unwittingly helped them hide the coins. The Ute chief, Towaoc, led a raiding party on a rampage of their own and killed and scalped the rogue Spaniards. The thing is though, the local Spanish priest, Father Miguel, was innocently riding with those rogues to show them the shortest way to find the Santa Fe trail.

Father Miguel had rescued Towaoc when he was a young orphan and helped raise him. He was, in effect, Towaoc's surrogate father. In the Ute killing frenzy Father Miguel was also scalped. He later died of his wounds. So 'Canyon of Tears' certainly earned its name."

Roger and Michael were silent. They had both been toughened by their respective combat duties but began to feel a growing respect for the Wahatoya.

Michael didn't want to completely divide his forces. He sent Special Agents Randy Ferguson and Tommy Roberts with Sven. Special Agent Brian King stayed behind. Michael knew to expect the unexpected, especially when the stakes were so high and he wanted Agent King close. All three of the agents were veteran commandos who had been trained by the legendary William Fairbairn and had served with the Royal Navy Commandos. After a few missions that would have defined the entire careers for many soldiers, the three were recruited by the FBI. They were "on loan" from the U.S. Navy to work on special assignments with Michael. Michael's assignments were a hodge-podge of intelligence, counter-intelligence, dirty tricks, financial espionage and advising the president on very sensitive issues like the Los Alamos defector. Very little disturbed Michael these days but learning about the secrets that Daniel Frost was trying to carry to the Germans shook him to his very core. He had received a crash course in the Manhattan Project, which was scary enough, but the thought of Hitler building a weapon capable of such horrific destruction was unthinkable. Michael had also seen intelligence reports that Germany was very close to developing a long range bomber that could reach the U.S. He shuddered at the possibilities. Michael believed that just telling the agents that Daniel Frost was "very important" was not enough. He was teetering on the edge of his authority when he divulged what he knew about Frost's secrets, but he wanted them to understand the import of their mission.

Canyon of Tears

Willie, like his rider Sven, was weathered and worn. The sheriff had sent him because he was the best mountain horse in the valley. Willie was closing in on twenty years, which made him a senior citizen. But he was sure-footed and had the best trail instincts of any horse Sven had ever ridden. Sven assumed that he would have to babysit the two FBI agents so he was pleasantly surprised when each of them expertly threw a saddle on his horse, cinched it down tightly and slipped the bridle in with ease. They were in their saddles waiting for Sven. Without a word Sven headed for a line of trees. The pack horse fell in line behind him and agents Ferguson and Robertson followed.

The terrain changed almost immediately into a noticeable incline. The tall pines cast giant shadows across the riders' path, darkening the whiteness of the snow. The canyon was a true geological wonder. The floor was narrow and winding. The walls on both sides were covered with trees and other foliage and the surface of the walls alternated between peaks and valleys, almost undulating like waves of a green and leafy sea. It was easy to see why snow never reached the canyon floor. The tall pines and firs stretched their long branches and acted as barriers.

naiku

Sven couldn't help reminiscing about riding his first pony in this canyon. By the time he was fourteen years old, he had been accepted as a fixture in the Ute band's daily life. At first the young braves were merciless with their teasing. They all wanted to prove their fighting prowess at his expense. Sven never once backed down from a challenge. As he grew stronger and taller his fighting skills improved and before long he could hold his own against their best fighters. There were no grownups to intercede or to protect him. He developed a reputation as a punishing fighter, one who would never quit, no matter how badly hurt. He never stopped coming after his opponent and would inflict as much pain as possible. Soon the braves decided that the pain of fighting with Sven was simply not worth it.

Riding a borrowed pony, he had set out on his first riding lesson through the Canyon of Tears. The lesson was conducted mostly by the pony, every time he threw Sven to the ground. The young braves, who yelled encouragement and laughed loudly whenever Sven was sent sprawling, had a great time. Slowly the lesson turned into Sven teaching the pony that he was not about to give up. The two of them then became a great team. Eventually Sven traded several beaver pelts to make the pony his very own.

It was only a matter of time before Sven became "one of the boys." Their childhood games turned into hunting trips with the older braves, who instructed them in the ways of the forest and gave them menial jobs to do. One day Sven was asked if he wanted to ride with a raiding party to steal horses from a small band of Apaches who were camping nearby. Sven had hesitated because he was not comfortable with the Ute practice of stealing horses. Since two of his friends were going, though, he decided to ride along. He was the junior member of the raiding party, so Sven was given the task of holding the Ute horses out of sight and keeping them quiet and relaxed while the others slipped into the sleeping Apaches' camp and grabbed as many horses as they could. That suited him fine because he loved handling the horses and they behaved well around him. Old Sai'-ar had taught him a chant to soothe and relax the horses. Staying with the horses might appear to be menial but a raiding party could turn into disaster if the waiting horses became spooked and ran away or if they became agitated or frightened and panicked when the braves returned, often with the enemy in hot pursuit. It was not a time for the warriors (or thieves in this case) to be struggling with their horses when immediate departure was called for. Ute braves often left their horses hidden while they sneaked into an enemy's camp. The chance of stealth and surprise was much better on foot. Sven held the lead ropes (the Utes did not use bridles) of the ten horses. He softly chanted the song Sai'-ar had taught him.

Sven sang the verse to the horses over and over as he stroked their foreheads and occasionally fed them handfuls of corn. The plan was for the raiding party to sneak into the Apaches' camp, quietly steal as many horses as they could and sneak back out unnoticed. Sven first knew that the plan wasn't working when he heard distant shouting. The horses heard also. They began to tense and one of them pulled back against Sven's grip. He raised the volume of his chant slightly and moved closer to the offending horse. If he allowed panic to spread he couldn't possibly hold on to all of them. He reached out his hand

THE WAHATOYA   51

and soothingly patted the horse's nose. He could hear running footsteps and prepared himself for the chaos about to erupt. He would be the last one to mount because he needed to control each horse until its rider was mounted. Would the Apache pursuers be close behind? What had gone wrong? Sven stood his ground as pandemonium broke out. The Ute braves mounted their horses in a frenzy and yanked the ropes from Sven's grasp. Sven had to dodge hoofs as the horses exploded into gallops. Adding to the chaos were three stolen Apache horses. Finally the last rope was pulled from Sven's hand and he mounted his own horse on the run. Not knowing who might be behind him, he urged his pony through the darkness, navigating by the sounds of the thundering hooves ahead of him. After thirty minutes of hard riding the party slowed their horses and Sven caught up to them. The braves were drunk with excitement. Sven pieced together the story of the raid from the braves' excited chatter interspersed among their war whoops. They had gone undetected until the last minute when one of the liberated horses protested. The sleeping Apaches woke up and a fierce battle ensued. The Utes killed three of them and outran the rest. Since the Apaches were short of horses, they couldn't pursue the Utes with sufficient man power. The killing of the Apache braves was a distant, unseen event so it didn't bother Sven, but when one of the Utes held up a bloody scalp for Sven to admire it was like a sledge hammer had slammed into his stomach.

Sven had become quite the horseman after that. He tamed rather than "broke" many a wild horse for the tribe's remuda. He felt a kinship with horses and could often calm their jittery nerves. Sven also learned just how important were horses to the Ute Indians. They traded horses to the Spanish settlement and to the Spaniards passing through on their way to the Santa Fe Trail so the horses were an integral part of their economy. They relied on fast and strong horses for hunting. Without them the tribe would starve to death. Horses provided status to their tribe and to their chief thereby improving their sense of well being in their world.

Sven remembered vividly that the raiding party had ridden through the Canyon of Tears on the way back to their camp. That had been, what, sixty-five years ago? He had lost track of time.

Sven pulled up and dismounted. He led Willie to a small pool of water. Randy and Tommy followed with relief. Their legs and butts were feeling the effects of being in the saddle. The horses drank deeply then began nosing around the sparse grass peeking out of the shadows.

"We'll rest the horses for a few minutes," Sven offered.

"How much longer to the summit?" Randy asked.

"We're not actually going to the summit, at least not at first. Just beyond timber line there's an open area that will give us a good view of the peak and the entire side of the mountain. I'm hoping that we can spot signs of the crash from there. If that's the case, we can head directly to the crash instead of climbing all the way to the top and then backtracking to the site. We have another three hours of riding and walking before we camp."

The two agents just nodded. They wondered what it was like for their fellow agents on that mountain.

naiku

The first night on the mountain had been a living hell. Ben's scalp wound was pulsating with pain, making it almost impossible for him to sleep. When he did drift off to sleep it was to dream of the screams of his crewmen, who seemed to be trapped somewhere in the airplane that Ben had just crashed. He could never find them. All he could do was to listen to them scream for help. When he thought he had located one of them, it turned out to be his passenger, Daniel. Daniel spent most of the first night screaming in pain. All Ben could do was melt snow and give him water. He kept him covered. He checked the splint and loosened the bindings. Daniel was delirious part of the time and babbled in German. Ben ventured outside just long enough to gather fire wood and to collect snow to melt into water. Under the trees the snow was not nearly as deep and he could navigate quite well. He also left the plane to get away from Daniel's suffering. Maybe he should start walking. Maybe he would meet up with the rescuers. But he knew he couldn't bring himself to abandon Daniel or his crew members. *Which ones were real and which ones were in his dreams?* Ben was confused. He couldn't think straight. His injury, lack of sleep and the lack of oxygen at the high altitude were eating away at his ability to function. A fire—that's what he needed. He would build a fire because he knew some one would be searching for the wreck.

Ben had to hike some distance to locate wood large enough to build a signal fire. Each time he dragged a fallen limb into the open and stacked it on the growing pile he had to sit down and rest. He was gasping for air. After a couple of hours he was exhausted but he had a sizeable pile of dead wood. The shadows were growing longer and Ben was determined to light the signal fire before dark. If searchers were anywhere near, they would see the flame. He rummaged around the broken wing and located one of the fuel tanks that remained intact. Ben poked a small hole in the tank and quickly inserted the end of a rubber tube he had cut away from the fuselage. He pointed the other end of the tube into a makeshift metal container. The fuel flowed freely and quickly filled it up. He crimped the rubber tube and secured it against the fuel tank with the end pointed upward so the fuel could not leak out. He might need more.

Ben walked around the wood pile, splashing fuel around the bottom and into its center. He stuffed a variety of combustible material from the airplane's interior in between the stacked wood. Returning to the plane's interior, he built a crude torch. He didn't want to risk lighting a match outdoors for fear it would blow out before he could ignite the fire. The plane's survival kit contained one box of wooden matches. Ben wrapped gauze and cotton balls together and loosely covered them with some dry cloth and taped it all together over and around the end of a large, broken branch. He rubbed the head of his makeshift torch around the inside of his empty fuel carrier, from where it soaked up the remaining fuel. The match lit on the first try and Ben ignited his torch. He had a robust flame instantly. By the time he had walked out to the stack of dead wood, his torch handle had caught fire and was popping loudly. Ben walked around the perimeter of the stack and applied fire to its base in several spots. The fire caught eagerly and was soon roaring. Sparks flew high into the sky and the flames threw eerie shadows onto the soft snow. The heat of the flames touched Ben and he reveled in the warmth. He felt like he had been cold for days. Mesmerized, he stared at the flames. He felt like they were drawing him in. Maybe if he followed their siren song his soul would escape this place along with the glowing embers that spiraled out of sight. But the positive act of building the fire seemed to spark a tiny ray of hope.

Maybe we do have a chance to survive this, he thought.

Mountain SOS

Heil Hitler

"This is Sheriff Dunn," Lonnie answered his ringing phone.

"Hey, Lonnie. This Joe Cordova in Trinidad." Joe was the sheriff of Las Animas County. "What's the status of your search and rescue for that missing plane?"

Lonnie Dunn hesitated. Normally he and the neighboring law enforcement types readily shared any and all information they had. But the appearance of FBI agents and mysterious men who carried the President's signature around in their pockets made him nervous. "Hold on a minute, Joe." He covered the mouth piece. "It's the sheriff over in Trinidad. Wants to know about our search and rescue mission." That a plane was missing was not a secret. It turned out that several ranchers had heard the engines and the minute strangers came to town it wasn't hard to figure out. Michael nodded to the sheriff.

"Well, Sven Curry is leading the team. They left early this morning on horseback. Why do you ask? You got any information on the plane?"

"Nothing about the plane crash, but I just found out from Ernie over at the General Store that two strangers came into his store yesterday and bought a lot of cold weather gear. He tried to talk to them, but they wouldn't say a word. Then Chris Hopkins, the snowplow driver, asked me if I knew anything about a couple of hunters he saw on horseback up near Apishapa Pass. I was pretty sure that you had already put together a search team from your side."

Lonnie then asked him, "What made Chris think they were hunters?"

"Well, he told me that they had rifles strapped on."

"Thanks for the call Joe. I'll let you know if I find out anything." Lonnie put the phone down and looked at Michael. "I think we've got a problem." He re-told Joe Cordova's story. Michael turned pale. "Oh, my God," he exhaled. Michael asked for some privacy and called Washington D.C. He spoke to several different men who served in several different agencies and capacities. Many of them called him back over the next couple of hours. Michael sometimes interrupted them with questions and then listened intently while shaking his head. He finally called in Roger and the sheriff.

"Problem?" Roger asked.

Michael deliberated just a moment. He had to bring these two into his confidence. The stakes were too high not to use every single resource he had.

"We have one bitch of a problem. Those strangers are almost certainly members of a very elite, top secret agency deep within Germany's Waffen SS. The group is known as The Death Heads. They are highly trained assassins. Hitler uses them for the dirtiest of his dirty work. Our intelligence folks believe that they came to the U.S. by way of a merchant ship that docked in Newfoundland a couple of weeks ago. Mountains and snow mean nothing to them. They are experts at navigation. They will find that crash. They were probably sent over to smuggle our Los Alamos defector back to Germany. They would have been monitoring his movements. They may even have another contact at Los Alamos who fed them the information that he was put on board the airplane. Our search and rescue team are dead men if we don't warn them."

naiku

Special Agents Randy Ferguson and Tommy Roberts were gasping for air. They had dismounted and left the horses an hour ago. The trail was just too rocky and too steep to continue on horseback. The agents were desperately trying to keep up with Sven as he nimbly picked his way over the loose shale. They had left the trees and foliage behind when the trail meandered out of the canyon. The vista was magnificent. They could see for miles in all directions. The vastness of the snow covered peak just ahead of them was visually overpowering. Sven looked back at them and stopped to let them catch up. Once they were together, Sven squatted down. It was impossible not to notice that he was not even breathing hard. The two agents gratefully sat and concentrated on breathing for a minute. The altitude was slightly over eleven thousand feet and the oxygen was at a premium. Sven was studying the looming mountainside through binoculars, searching for any sign of the wreckage or the crash site.

"We only have a couple of hours before dark, so we need to hurry. I want to camp on that outcropping." Sven pointed up the mountain. "It's fairly level and there's some protection from the wind. Be sure and drink plenty of water from here on." Sven was already moving. The agents scrambled to their

THE WAHATOYA 57

feet and adjusted their packs. Their sudden movement caused a commotion among three furry guests, who had been sitting close by, intently watching their every move. The marmots scurried a safe distance away. They chattered noisily at the strange intruders and shadowed them as they climbed higher and higher.

By the time they reached the camp site, the agents' legs were trembling and their lungs were crying for air. It took fifteen minutes for them to regain their normal breathing cycle. There would be no fire. Their evening meal consisted of beef jerky and water. When the agents finished eating they curled up in their sleeping bags and immediately fell asleep. Not even the brilliant night sky could distract them this night. Sven watched the darkening mountain. There! He swung his binoculars up. There was no doubt about it. Someone had built a large fire. That meant there was at least one survivor.

The horizon was showing the first blush of dawn when Sven woke the FBI agents. They immediately set about rolling up their sleeping bags. Sven wanted to travel light so he had not allowed even coffee cups. They chugged water and hastily ate their morning beef jerky. They felt a renewed sense of urgency now that they knew someone was alive and waiting for them.

"Sven, look." Randy Ferguson was pointing up the mountain. Sven and Tommy strained their eyes against the growing brightness of daylight. "There, I see it," Sven was pointing at a large plume of black smoke rising into the thin air. It took a savvy (and clear thinking) survivor to remember to burn materials that produced black smoke during the day. It was easier to see from a distance, especially against a background of snow. They headed up the mountain, their snowshoes crunching through the snow's crusty surface.

naiku

The revived bonfire buoyed Ben's spirits. He piled more debris from the wreckage on the flames. The black smoke curled upward. At least he was doing something. He had slept better and so had Daniel. Daniel's pain seemed to have subsided somewhat. Ben had boiled pine needles in water and told Daniel that it was soup. That seemed to raise his spirits. Daniel had told Ben who he was and why he had been arrested by the FBI. Ben was speechless. He had heard rumors of a massively destructive weapon being developed by the United States but had reckoned that it would get bogged down in some bureaucratic boondoggle and never be finished. Now he finds out that his passenger was a physicist who had been working on the bomb and had been about to defect to Germany! Ben's first reaction had been, *Well, hell, I'll just shoot the traitor and save everybody the trouble.* But he knew he wouldn't do that. *It was one thing to drop thousands of pounds of bombs on the enemy from twenty—thousand feet and quite another to be looking them in the eye when you pulled the trigger. Wasn't it?*

Ben's flight to and from Ploesti had been a gut wrenching, adrenalin pumping, death defying trip. He had been as close to death as you could get but never once did it cross his mind that he was going to die. Now surrounded by the solitude of the mountain and rendered virtually powerless by circumstances, he feared his own death. He imagined that it was stalking him, lurking outside the broken fuselage waiting for the right moment to pounce on him. It saddened him to think that there would be no family to grieve over his death or to pray for him. He wondered if he would see his departed mother or if death was just forever darkness and nothingness. The thought of meeting his mother in some kind of heaven lightened his mood slightly.

A Pact with the Devil

As it turned out, Daniel and his family were German Jews. Daniel was a brilliant young graduate student working under the tutelage of Enrico Fermi when the Nobel Prize winner fled to the United States to escape the growing fascism in Europe. He had convinced Daniel to come with him to the University of Chicago. Daniel would send for his parents later. But Hitler's SS had arrested his parents along with thousands of other German Jews and sent them to a concentration camp. Daniel's horror grew as he heard and read about the Jews' plight. His parents would have been gassed early on if it had not been for one of Daniel's former professors who now advised the Nazis on their own version of a doomsday weapon. The professor had recognized his parents' name and suggested that better use might be made of this family than to incinerate them.

naiku

On the way to his lab one morning, Daniel was handed a brown paper bag by a stranger and told in passing, "Look at the contents carefully and do not tell anyone. You will be contacted later." Later, when Daniel was eating his lunch, he carefully pulled two photographs from the bag. After ensuring that he was alone, he spread the photos out before him. He gasped, then emitted a low, guttural moan. His very soul cried out. At first he turned his eyes away to escape the horrible images. *No one should have to look at photos like this. Who would take such photos? Did such animals exist in this world?* He wanted to cry out but stifled his anguish. He needed to be sure what he was seeing. This time he studied the nude photos of his mother and father. They had obviously been separated from the crowd of nude men and women, and *Oh, my God!* children lined up in front of a long, low building. The agony on their faces tore at Daniel's heart. The next photo showed them standing in front of a long mass grave, in which had been piled hundreds of dead bodies.

60   GARY L. BRIDGES

Two days later he was followed by the same man who had delivered the photos. The man came up to his small apartment. As soon as the door clicked shut behind him, he spoke to Daniel.

"Your parents are still alive because the Nazis want you to do a job for them. The moment you falter or if you tell anyone, they will be gassed and will die horrible deaths. Do you understand?" the stranger looked at Daniel coldly.

"Yes," Daniel stammered, choking back tears. "Please don't hurt them. I'll do anything you ask."

"Good. Now listen carefully. Memorize this set of instructions. If you miss any of the delivery dates or are late for a delivery, the agreement will be null and void and your parents will be placed back in the general population and will be taken to the chambers. As long as you cooperate they will continue to be well-fed and clothed."

Daniel was trembling as he memorized addresses and routes and delivery dates. When he handed the paper back the stranger burned it, and rolled the ashes up in another sheet of paper and stuck it in his pocket. From then on Daniel passed along information about the work that he was doing with Fermi. If the Americans caught him he would probably be executed as a traitor or spy (would it matter which?). Then his parents would die also. Would they know in their last moments that he, their son, had failed them?

The stranger had followed him to Los Alamos and had told him that it was time for him to return to Germany where he would work for Werner Eisenberg, Germany's chief nuclear scientist. Eisenberg thought that with the formula Daniel was smuggling out of the United States, Germany could develop the Atomic Bomb before the Americans. Eisenberg planned to test the new weapon on London.

naiku

Ben was dumbfounded. *How could this happen to me?* he agonized. *This poor guy is going to lose his parents because I crashed my airplane. If he escapes, I'll probably be guilty of treason, or worse!* Ben yearned for the plain-vanilla bombing raids over enemy territory where the objectives were very straight forward: kill the enemy and blow up all their shit. Ben kept his thoughts to himself and gave Daniel some water. He was afraid to look too closely at the broken leg but he steeled himself and looked anyway. It was still swollen but the color of the leg above and below the break still looked good. That meant that his circulation was okay. Ben had worried that the blood flow to Daniel's foot would be restricted, which could result in his losing the foot.

THE WAHATOYA

naiku

"Captain Ben Curtis. This is Special Agent Randy Ferguson, FBI. Can you hear me?" The agent's booming voice echoed across the craggy expanse of mountain and rock.

Rescued

"You look like hell, son," Sven told Ben when they were face to face. Ben's hair was matted with dried blood. He had smudges of blood on his forehead and cheeks. His eyes were sunken and bloodshot. He tried to laugh at Sven's declaration but broke down crying instead.

"I . . . I'm sorry. I'm, I'm just glad to see you." Ben struggled to regain his composure. Agent Ferguson handed him a canteen. Ben drank deeply. Randy then gave him his beef jerky.

"Are there any other survivors?" Randy asked him. Ben looked at him.

"Just one. The prisoner survived. All the others are dead." Ben turned and they all followed him into the wreckage. Ben led them to each of the agent's body. "I'm sorry. I didn't know what to do about the bodies." Randy Ferguson put his hand on Ben's shoulder and squeezed.

"Don't worry. We'll take care of them." He and Agent Tommy Roberts began moving pieces of wreckage to free the bodies of their fellow agents and friends. They had been here before, recovering bodies of fallen comrades. It was a dark, sorrowful place and they never demeaned the task as "just part of the job." It was more than that and it hurt like hell.

Sven looked at the clumsily built splint on Daniel's broken leg. By not changing anything, Sven paid Ben his ultimate, though silent, compliment.

It took the FBI agents about an hour to free the bodies. They laid them out on the snow, each one covered with a piece of torn canvas or some article of clothing. The mood was somber. Sven had built a crude but sturdy litter on which to carry Daniel. Much like the travois used by the Ute Indians to transport the sick or injured, it had two extended handles, typically tied on each side of a horse. Sven had constructed it so that a man could pull it. Later, he would adapt it for a horse. Ben told Agent Ferguson that he had unlocked Daniel's shackles so that he could treat his injury.

"Don't worry about it. You did what you had to do," Randy assured him. Ben struggled with whether or not to reveal what he knew about Daniel's family and background. He decided to keep it to himself. It wouldn't change what they had to do. Daniel could tell them the story for himself. Sven was pushing them to get started down the mountain. The two agents huddled and discussed how to handle the bodies of the dead agents. It was apparent that they could not transport any bodies. Their mission was to secure and deliver the prisoner and beyond that get any other survivors home alive. The dead would have to wait for another day. They stacked the bodies inside the wreckage alongside the B-24 crewmembers and blocked the access as best they could to deter roving wildlife. A recovery team would come later.

It was mid-afternoon before they were ready to head down the mountain. Sven would lead the way. Agent Ferguson would start out pulling the litter and Daniel. Ben would follow him and Agent Roberts would take up the rear. They planned to spend the night at the prior camp site. Ben had leaned over to secure the snow shoes to his boots when he heard a loud "Ummph." He stood up just in time to see Randy Ferguson fly backwards. He landed on his back with a resounding thump.

"What . . . . ?" Barely a split second later, he heard the unmistakable crack of rifle fire. Before Ben could react Tommy Roberts slammed into him, knocking him to the ground. Ben heard the deadly crack of the rifle as he hit the ground. "Agent Roberts, are you okay?" Ben squirmed his way out from under the agent's body. Ben felt for a pulse. There was nothing. He looked around for Sven. Sven was flat on the ground next to Randy Ferguson, trying to find a sign of life. The agent was dead. Ben reached into Tommy Roberts' coat and located his pistol. He pulled it out and crawled over to Sven. Ben found Randy's pistol and removed it.

"Do you think that's some hunter who is mistaking us for game?" Ben breathed to Sven.

"No, those were two different rifles and they knew what they were firing at."

"They came for me." Daniel spoke up.

"What? How can you be sure?"

"They've been watching me ever since they started blackmailing me. I just had no idea they would come up the mountain for me. I would have said something. I swear I would." Daniel covered his face with both hands.

Sven looked at Ben. Ben told him, "The FBI was afraid that Daniel was going to carry secrets from Los Alamos to give to the Germans. It has something to do with a new bomb being built. My crew was supposed to deliver him to Pueblo."

Together they crawled over to Daniel and pulled him over next to the wreckage, which offered a wall of protection.

"We'll wait until dark to start down the mountain. If we can get to the canyon, we have a good chance of staying ahead of them." Sven told Ben and Daniel. Daniel didn't respond. Ben was thinking that Daniel must feel like the loneliest man on earth.

Sven surveyed the mountain for signs of activity. It wasn't too hard to figure out the direction of the two shots. The question was, how far away were the shooters? Sven supposed that they had specially-made sniper rifles with powerful scopes. They could have made the shots as far away as a mile he supposed. If that was the case, they had a good head start. He didn't harbor any illusions that he would outsmart them by traveling at night. There was little doubt that men like these would not stop to sleep when their prey was on the run.

The moon was on their side. The thin sliver of orange that rose above East Peak provided a magnificent spectacle but produced little light. Sven pulled Daniel's litter. He had given Ben a cursory lesson in how to walk with snow shoes and let him take up the rear. He couldn't get lost, even in the dark, because the litter left such a wide and distinctive trail in the snow. Sven wanted to cover their tracks but speed was more important than stealth tonight.

Ben found that walking with snow shoes was exhausting. He fell several times and struggled to get himself upright again. Then he had to hurry even more to make up the lost ground. At one point, Sven and Daniel were out of sight and Ben momentarily panicked. He pushed hard and caught sight of them. His lungs felt like they would burst. His heart was pounding and every beat sent ripples of pain through the laceration in his scalp. Ben's toes were numb from the wet cold seeping through his boots. By dawn Ben was well out of sight of Sven. He was stumbling by then. His snow shoes became tangled and he fell face first in the snow. He was exhausted. He could not get to his feet. Maybe Sven could at least save Daniel and turn him over to the FBI.

Well, I guess my luck ran out over Ploesti. God, I just wish I could have saved my crew. And this boondoggle—they didn't deserve to die on the top of a mountain because I didn't turn on the de-icing equipment, he thought.

"Come on. I need your help. You can't die on me, not yet." Sven put his arms under Ben's arm pits and pulled him up. He put Ben's right arm over his shoulder and let him lean into Sven. The combination of step-shuffle resulted in a strange gait but it worked. They were only a hundred yards from the entrance to the Canyon of Tears. Sven had hidden Daniel and gone

Escape

back for Ben. The horses were grazing nearby. Willie knew not to wander off and besides, there was still grass inside the canyon and he didn't want to fight the snow.

By the time the sun was peeking over East Peak, the beleaguered men were well hidden from view in the canyon. Sven went out with an armful of fir branches he had cut and tried to sweep the snow over their tracks. If he could erase their tracks, perhaps the Nazis would not find the entrance to the canyon.

The Hunters

Unbeknownst to Ben Curtis, he had unwittingly signaled the wrecked plane's whereabouts to the two Germans when he lit the large bonfire. Oh, they would have found it eventually. They always found their prey. It would have taken them a little longer but they would have found it. Arndt and Dietmar had served together since being recruited into the Jungsturm Adolf Hitler in 1925. They were fifteen years old at the time. The Hitler Youth underwent several transformations and reorganizations and by 1926 was renamed Hitler-Jugend, League of German Worker Movement. By 1930, there were over twenty-five thousand boys aged fourteen and upwards enlisted. The junior branch enlisted boys aged ten to fourteen years old. These boy-recruits were seen as future "Aryan supermen" and were steeped in anti-Semitism. The purpose was to instill in them the motivation to fight as soldiers for the Third Reich. Their early training emphasized military training over academic study. In 1933 Baldur von Schirach became the first Reich Youth Leader. He set out to identify boys who exhibited above average intellect and leadership qualities as well as superb military skills. These young men were sent to advanced training, which included special operations, intelligence gathering, extreme physical training, tactical operations and advanced survival skills. Arndt and Dietmar excelled in every aspect of their training. They also were among an even more elite group, which had absolutely no moral or ideological ambivalence about killing. Their allegiance to Hitler's twisted political and social demagoguery was limitless and they had no fear. The training and indoctrination these men had received for over half of their entire lives gave them a deadly advantage over any commando or special agent that the United States could send against them. Michael was one of the few Americans who understood the extent of this frightening and lethal gap.

Michael's intelligence sources were certain that, based on intercepted radio messages and a top secret communication from a mole deep within Hitler's circle of military commanders, Germany had sent two of their deadliest operatives to bring Daniel to Germany. Michael had an unknown number of FBI agents (some of who were probably injured or dead by now), a small town sheriff and an eighty-year old rancher/used-to-be Indian for a combat team. There was no time to get reinforcements from Washington. Michael had a deep foreboding about what lay ahead, for the survivors and for the search team. There was no choice. He had to lead another team up the mountain.

naiku

Sven took Ben about a hundred yards into the canyon. He sat him down, then pulled some heavy fir branches away from a slight indentation in the canyon wall and uncovered Daniel, who was still in the litter and had been hidden by the limbs. Ben breathed heavily for a few minutes. Sven sat next to him.

"I get the feeling that whoever is tracking us is very good at what they do and that they won't hesitate to kill us. It's only a matter of time before they figure out that we didn't continue down the mountain. They'll backtrack and keep looking until they find the entrance to this canyon and they'll come for us. We can't out-gun them but we can out smart them. We'll travel about another half-mile on horse back and then we're going to climb out of the canyon." Sven nodded his head toward the canyon wall. He rose to his feet and began preparing the horses for the trip. Sven secured Daniel's litter handles to each side of the pack horse so the horse could pull the litter. Ben and Sven would ride horseback. Sven didn't dare let them waste time sleeping. He wanted to get out of the canyon before daybreak. Ben had ridden horses as a young boy on his family's farm but he could always see where he was going. It was unsettling to ride in the dark but he trusted Sven and followed his advice to just give the horse his head. Sven, riding Willie, took the lead. Willie was sure-footed and stepped carefully as he felt his way in the dark. They rode for about an hour. Finally Sven stopped and dismounted. "We're here," he explained as his foot hit the ground. Ben dismounted and bent over Daniel to check on him. "How're you doing?"

"I'm alright. The jostling hurt a little, but I'm just glad to be on the move. What are we doing next?"

"I'm not real sure but Sven seems to have a plan."

Sven was emptying a leather bag tied to the pack horse. He laid several ropes on the ground. Ben asked, "Can I help with anything?"

"Start carrying these ropes over there—next to the wall." Sven pointed the way.

THE WAHATOYA   69

He then criss-crossed a rope under and over Daniel and the litter several times, tying knots in strategic locations, until he had manufactured a web virtually encasing the litter. A single rope strand emerged from the maze in the center, about a foot above the top of Daniel. Daniel looked like a package bound up for delivery. Sven then tied a make-shift rope harness around Ben's chest. He told Ben to pull Daniel and the litter next to the wall. Sven then filled Willie's saddlebags with rocks. When they were full, Sven loosely tied two logs loosely and hung them over the saddle, a log resting on each side of Willie's saddle.

"A trained, experienced tracker will notice a difference in the horses' hoof prints. The difference being that one moment the horses were carrying weight and the next moment they were not. If we can get them to stay on the horses' trail until they exit the canyon, we'll gain valuable time. Once again they'll have to backtrack looking for our trail. That's why we have to go there." He pointed up the canyon wall.

"In the dark?" Ben asked incredulously.

"Don't worry. I'll go first. I know the way. It's an old Ute trick. I've seen a small band of Utes lift horses out of a canyon using a system of rope pulleys. I'll go to the top and tie the knots and make the pulleys. I'll pull Daniel's litter. After it leaves the ground wait about thirty minutes then start climbing, using the second rope for support. Don't worry. I have a fail-safe system that will keep tension on your rope. All you have to do is to keep climbing. It'll take about an hour because I'll be constantly adjusting the ropes, tying them off at various locations and regulating the home-made pulleys." With that word of encouragement, Sven started his climb. He had three of the long ropes draped over his shoulders. Ben thought that they must have added about fifty pounds to Sven's load. The wall was not straight up (it bowed in and then out) and there were several large trees growing out of the wall; Sven had help from the landscape but it was a grueling trek. He allowed the longest rope to unwind as he climbed. The end of that rope lay on the canyon floor. Another rope was tied to the web encasing the litter. It took him almost an hour to reach the top of the canyon wall. Even though he was sweating and breathing heavily, he set to work immediately. He worked quickly and efficiently, running the ropes over tree limbs and tying a series of rope pulleys designed to use the least effort to raise the litter out of the canyon. Sven soon tied the anchor rope for Ben to pull/climb out of the canyon.

Ben watched the litter rise jerkily off the canyon floor. It soon disappeared into the darkness and Ben began his internal clock. He started up the wall. At first the ascent was fairly mild and he barely needed the rope but it soon turned into a pull-fest that took every ounce of strength. He had to stop and rest every time the topography allowed it. His shoulders and arms were aching. Just when Ben thought he couldn't continue, Sven had raised Daniel to the top and was able to pull Ben's rope, giving him a much needed boost.

Sven had been right. His misdirection tactic had led the Germans away from the canyon entrance and down the mountain, but not for long. In fact, if it had been daylight the ruse would not have worked. The Germans realized that they had been fooled and turned around. The steep climb in knee-high snow slowed them down considerably though. It was daylight before they discovered the swept-over tracks. It took them another hour of exploring and back-tracking to find the canyon entrance. By that time Ben had made it to the top and they had pulled up the ropes. Arndt and Dietmar grudgingly accepted that they were chasing a very worthy opponent. They found the hoof prints and set out on a steady pace of pursuit. They were determined not to be fooled again. They found the trail easy to follow because there was only one way through the canyon. Nevertheless it took the better part of an hour for them to reach the canyon entrance. Beyond the canyon's front door lay an open meadow. The Germans didn't want to expose themselves so Arndt climbed a tall leaning fir tree to survey the landscape. Using the powerful binoculars, he spotted the Americans' horses pawing the fresh snow. Their efforts provided a tasty meal for the horses and a surprising visual treat—patches of green grass poking through the white snow.

"ScheiBel"! Arndt cursed. He half slid and half climbed out of the tree. He explained to Dietmar what he had seen; the horses with the weights still on their saddles and no riders in sight. They argued for a moment. It was an uncharacteristic outburst for both of them. They realized that, once again, their targets had out-foxed them. Dietmar wanted to back track and locate the spot where the survivors had left the canyon. Even "Aryan supermen", though, had their limits. The Germans had been awake for over fifty hours and they had been pushing themselves beyond imagination. Their bodies and their minds were beginning to shut down from exhaustion. They hid themselves in a well concealed recess of the canyon wall. It was about twelve feet above the floor and hidden by foliage and rocks. The killers slept.

The hunt would have to wait.

Willie's Masquerade

Rescuing the Rescuers

Michael agonized over the rag-tag rescue (or would it turn out to be a recovery?) team. Sheriff Joe Cordova had joined them at Sheriff Dunn's request. It would be the two sheriffs plus himself and the FBI agent, Brian King.

"Joe has dealt with his share of bad guys." Sheriff Dunn had told Michael. He hesitated and then added, "He's put more than his share of them in their graves."

Michael wanted to tell both of these dedicated lawmen that he had probably sentenced them all to death by undertaking this mission. No one but perhaps Brian King fully understood the nature of the Nazis and their fanaticism. The Nazi's potential threat to the United States was horrifying. Michael knew that he had to do whatever was necessary, including taking whatever risks were necessary, to stop the Germans from taking the Los Alamos defector to Germany.

Special Agent Brian King un-wrapped his sniper rifle. Technically it was known as the Lee-Enfield Rifle No. 4 Mk1 and was manufactured in the United States by the Savage-Stevens Firearms Company. To the very select group of FBI agents who had received sniper training, the rifle was commonly referred to as the "head hunter." The FBI had contracted with the Savage-Stevens Firearms Company to modify the standard issue rifle into a true long-distance sniper rifle. They had designed a powerful new side-fitting scope so that the shooter could easily use either the standard iron sight or the scope. By tweaking the length and the interior of the barrel and using an innovative metal alloy, the designers had produced a much stronger barrel that could deliver an onslaught of bullets over a much greater distance. It was the use of this weapon that enabled snipers to proclaim "one shot, one kill." Agent King was the best marksman in the FBI and that meant he may have been the best marksman anywhere. He was no slouch with his hand gun either. Unlike Michael, Agent King was eagerly anticipating hunting down the two Nazis. He had been privy to much of the intelligence about Hitler's "final

THE WAHATOYA   73

solution" for the Jews. He knew what was happening in the concentration camps and he was furious that those "Nazi bastards" had the nerve to violate American soil. For Special Agent King there would be no hesitation about killing them. He relished the thought of the chase.

naiku

The second search party pulled their horse trailers into the field adjoining the entrance of the hidden canyon. Sheriff Dunn had a feeling he could find it even after all these years.

"Uh, oh," Sheriff Dunn drew in his breath. "That's Willie over there grazing. Our boys must be in trouble."

Agent King got out of the truck with his binoculars and began sweeping the immediate area for signs of life.

"Everybody stay put while I get Willie. A bunch of strangers will get him all excited," Sheriff Dunn explained. He walked toward Willie, who raised his head to size up his visitor. The sheriff whistled and Willie began walking toward him. The other horses fell in line thinking that there might be some feed or hay in store for them. Indeed there was, and the sheriff tore off some handfuls of alfalfa hay.

"Sven used the horses as decoys," he explained as he began to unload the rocks and logs tied to Willie's saddle. He turned to Michael. "What's our next move?"

Michael looked at Special Agent King. "Brian, are you thinking what I'm thinking?"

Agent King replied, "We can't go barreling up that canyon without knowing how many bad guys are in there or where they are. I'll take a little recon trip. Sheriff, can I get into that canyon from the top?"

Sheriff Dunn thought for a minute. "Sure, but it's hard to find. The best landmark I can think of is a large Ponderosa pine tree that was struck by lightning several years ago. The entire bottom half is scorched. Due north of that tree, you'll find a partial rock dike, kind of like the one we passed on our way here. This one runs up and down the mountain. Climb on top of it and you'll be able to look down into the canyon. You can pick where you want to enter."

Agent King turned to Michael as he secured his pack. "There's also the chance that they're watching us right now."

Sheriff Dunn chimed in, "I was thinking that myself. Why don't I drive you to a more secluded drop off spot and point you in the right direction?"

"Okay, let's go. I'll use this to signal you when I know more." Brian held up his signal mirror. Michael nodded agreement.

Sheriff Dunn had spent almost as much time as Sven had on and around the Wahatoya so he was able to give Brian King precise and accurate directions.

"Good luck agent King." He shook his hand.

"Thanks Sheriff. See you when the shootin' starts." Brian grinned at him. Men in his and Michael's business often resorted to dark humor when setting off on dangerous missions.

Brian King's senses jumped to a higher level now that he was on a job. Alone in a strange place, hunting the bad guys was as good as it got. He would leave the search and rescue mission to others. He loved to pit his skills against the enemy's. He always believed that he could out wait, out track, out think and out shoot the best of them. But he was never careless or reckless. He knew his limits and had, on many occasions, backed away from confrontation. When he engaged the enemy, though, he was deadly.

He moved through the forest like a shadow and found the scorched tree after an hour. Another half hour's hike brought him to the rock wall. He scaled the wall expertly and silently. From the top he could see where the canyon opened up and curved away into thick underbrush. He found a suitable departure point and took one last look around before climbing down the wall. Brian tied a rope to a tree near the ground so he could cover it up and prepared it for rappelling down the canyon wall. With the rope positioned around his butt and secured to the tree, Brian stepped off backwards and dropped straight down. He slowed his descent when the wall curved outward and planted his feet on the sloping wall and continued his orderly descent, controlling the rate of descent by positioning the rope. When he was about twenty feet from the canyon floor he stopped and unwound himself from his rope. The slope of the wall was gentle enough for him to walk around if he held on to a tree branch or a bush growing out of the wall. He found a tree with large branches growing near the ground. After climbing around in the branches for a few minutes, Brian found a spot that allowed him to look both directions in the canyon. He needed to be certain that no one was waiting in ambush for them.

Most people think of snipers as sharpshooters. They certainly are expert marksmen but they are much more. Snipers are trained to get in and get out of their target's environment undetected. They become experts at camouflage and at stealth. They learn to wait; well beyond simple patience. They learn how to kill up close and personal as well as at a distance. Brian King had no doubts that the Germans had also been trained in those skills. They were here, weren't they?

THE WAHATOYA

naiku

Arndt woke up first. He opened his eyes and listened intently before moving. Dietmar sensed his waking and opened his eyes. They had been asleep for five hours and it was daylight. Dietmar used a long stick to separate some of the undergrowth that helped hide their position. Slowly they emerged from their modest sleeping chamber. Dietmar climbed up the wall where he could see both directions. He watched and listened. Satisfied, they regrouped and set out to backtrack into the canyon and try to find where the Americans had eluded them.

Brian King heard the rustle of fabric against long grass. He listened intently. He could hear cadence, one step, one step, two steps. There were two men walking toward his position. They were coming from the direction of the canyon entrance. He slowly turned his head to watch for them. He was in no danger of being spotted from the ground because he had very carefully covered his tracks. He was invisible to anyone from the canyon floor. Nevertheless, he slowed his breathing and concentrated on the spot where he expected to first see the Germans.

So that's what a Nazi bastard looks like up close, Brian thought. They certainly had the physiques of supermen. One was probably six feet two and the other at least that height. Even through their winter clothing, Brian could tell that they were muscular and fit. Their bearing was that of professional soldiers. Brian would not make the mistake of underestimating these two. He entertained the idea of killing them both now. *The opportunity may not present itself again*, he thought. First of all, they didn't know if they had comrades nearby and showing their hand now could be disastrous. Secondly, if they had caught up with Sven and the others and stashed them somewhere, their only chance of finding them was to follow the Germans. With all that was at stake, Brian knew that they needed to err on the side of caution and watch and follow for now. He watched them pass underneath his position. Brian waited an hour to make sure that they were out of hearing range and to ascertain that they were alone. He slipped out of the tree and quietly slid down the sloping canyon wall. Hugging the wall where he could and staying hidden in the under brush as much as he could, he worked his way to the canyon entrance. He climbed another tall fir tree for cover and so Michael could see his signal more easily. Brian pulled out his mirror and began flashing the customary alert to signal that he was about to send a message.

It was Joe Cordova's turn with the binoculars. He was scanning the mountainside looking for just this signal.

"I've got something," he announced.

Michael ran over and took the glasses. He was the only one who would be able to translate the series of flashes. He found the signal. Brian flashed the "message coming" signal twice more. Then he began the message. "Good guys not here. Bad guys here. Two on the move. One hour. Waiting. Full speed." He repeated the message three times to be sure some one had received it. When he was done, Michael used his mirror to flash back the message, "Coming." The exchange would never win awards for grammar or for its prose but it was effective. Brian had told Michael that the two Germans were moving, they were one hour ahead of them, and that Brian would wait where he was and that they could come in without fear of being ambushed. Michael had signaled him back that they were on their way.

naiku

Sven had almost misdirected the Germans but Arndt was just too good. He noticed a scuff mark on the rock portion of the canyon wall. It was where Daniel's litter had momentarily been hung up when Sven pulled him up. Ben had had to climb up and jostle it slightly to free it from an outcropping. The force had created a wide scuff mark in the lichen that covered the rock surface and it had left an uncharacteristic white spot. Once the Germans knew where to look, they found other indications that the Americans had climbed up the wall. They were accomplished climbers themselves and they made short work of climbing the canyon wall. At the top they found evidence of the ropes being tied around branches. They had previously seen the wide swath left in the snow by Daniel's litter and now were convinced that one of the Americans was injured and being carried. They began searching for the trail with a new admiration for their quarry.

They had no idea that they were vastly underestimating Sven.

Sven was glad to be at a lower elevation and out of the snow. It would be much more difficult for the Germans now. Sven was taking his weakening party over rock outcroppings and hard packed ground whenever possible to eliminate their tracks. Daniel was suffering. His moans had escalated to cries for relief. They were all exhausted and dehydrated. Sven had no idea how close their pursuers were so he assumed the worst and pushed even harder, afraid to stop for rest or water. Ben was falling farther and farther behind. He sometimes lost sight of Sven, who was still pulling Daniel's litter, but Sven would not let up. Better for one to fall back and be captured than all three of them. He had adopted the Ute's sometimes cruel pragmatism.

Sanctuary

As evening of the second day neared, they were approaching Sven's destination. He had been traveling in circles to throw off the Germans. It would be a temporary safe haven. Sven had no doubt that the Germans would eventually find them unless they got help. How soon would that help come? Would help come at all? Did the sheriff even know that they were being chased by maniacal Nazis? Normally, Sven would have hidden and watched to make sure that the enemy was not in a position to see him enter his hiding place. But there was too little time and Sven was betting that there were only two pursuers. He stopped and squatted on his heels, waiting for Ben to catch up. Daniel's raspy breathing sounded louder now, his eyes were closed and his face was covered with sweat. Ben arrived, breathing heavily. He sat next to Sven and caught his breath.

"Is this it?"

"It's close by. You should look closely at our surroundings so you could find it again. Who knows how this will play itself out." Sven went on to point out some prominent landmarks and gave Ben some general descriptions of the landscape, including compass points.

"Pick up as much firewood as you can carry," he instructed Ben as he straightened up. After one last lingering look in all directions, Sven headed out with Daniel in tow. Ben followed them. After about thirty minutes Sven stopped at the base of a long rock wall. He disappeared behind the wall. Ben followed again, but this time Sven and the litter were nowhere to be seen. Ben scrambled up a pile of small rocks but could find no trace of Sven or any clue as to where he might have hidden. He didn't dare call out. Sven had warned him time and time again to stay quiet because voices carried long distances in the mountains. He climbed back down and walked around to the front of the wall. About fifteen feet from the wall he turned around to look at it from a distance. There was Sven standing at the top of the wall. When Ben returned to the top he saw Sven standing in a hole that was hidden from view by a large, shrub-like bush. Sven then sat down and, facing the opening, scooted on his butt until his head disappeared. Ben followed Sven down a gradual incline, much like on a playground slide, into a dark abyss. The slide ended about ten feet below the entrance. Ben stood still while his eyes adjusted to the darkness. He noticed a dim glow coming from his left and could see Sven's outline moving that direction. He followed, extending his arms out in front and to the sides, feeling walls on either side as he shuffled/walked. A soft breeze wafted through the dark space. Slowly his eyes adjusted and he came to the source of the light. Sven was standing over Daniel. A candle flickered brightly on a low rock shelf. A horrible odor assaulted Ben's senses. He vaguely recognized it and his stomach turned.

"Gangrene," Sven said matter-of-factly. "That leg's got to come off right now or he's a dead man."

Ben gathered all his courage and came closer to look. The broken leg was horribly swollen and discolored. Red streaks shot up Daniel's leg.

We can't possibly amputate his leg. In a dark cave with no medication, no instruments, no doctor! What does he mean, "it's got to come off"? Ben's mind raced.

"Start a hot fire. I'll get some water and be right back." Sven left. Ben needed to rest. He needed to think about the situation. He looked at Daniel's face. It was covered with sweat. His breathing was shallow and rough. Ben picked up the candle and turned around in the small room. Sven must have used this place before. There were a few pieces of scrap wood piled against the wall. Ben began building a stack that would light easily. He broke up several of the small pieces for kindling and arranged them at the bottom. He used the candle to light a long, dry splinter and stuck the fiery point into the loose pile of kindling. It ignited and began to crackle. Ben's combat first aid training began to kick in. He took his knife blade and began to cut away Daniel's pant leg, exposing his entire leg.

"Please don't let him cut off my leg." Daniel seized Ben's arm and squeezed it hard. His eyes were wide and panic echoed in his voice.

"Daniel, you can't survive with that leg. It's gangrene. I'm sorry." Ben pried Daniel's fingers from his arm.

"Oh God." Daniel began sobbing. "What am I going to do?" His body shook.

Sven returned with a bucket of water.

"As soon as the fire makes coals, sweep them all together and put the water on to boil." Sven opened a leather pouch and extracted a dry root. He sat down and put the roots between two smooth rocks and began grinding them, turning the roots into a coarse powder. He also produced a ball of resin-like material and some green leaves. He gave Ben a small tin cup and told him, "Put this resin in the cup and suspend the cup in the water after it starts boiling. Leave it until it melts. Okay?" He looked at Ben to see if he was up to the excruciating task ahead of them.

"Yeah, I understand." Ben put more wood on the flames. It wasn't too long before the blazing fire had produced a bed of red-hot coals. Sven lay the blade of his large hunting knife into the coals. His do-it-yourself pharmacy had produced a handful of brown, gritty-looking powder. Sven wet the end of his finger and stuck it into the concoction. Then he grabbed Daniel's upper lip, pulled it away from his gums and rubbed the grit onto Daniel's upper gum. He repeated the application on his lower gum.

"It'll act as a tranquilizer if it doesn't kill him. He won't be completely out but it will dull the pain and he'll be in another place for most of the time." Sven then checked on the heating water and the melting resin, which had gone soft and gooey. He mixed in the ground-up leaves and left it in the heating cup.

"Ben, I need you to keep him as still as possible. Sit on his chest and hold his arms in tightly. It's going to take me a good part of an hour to get his leg off."

Ben was sweating and his hands were shaking. "I'll take care of it," he whispered.

Sven removed his blade from the small furnace. The blade was as sanitized as he could get it. Anyway, infection would probably be the least of Daniel's worries. Ben straddled Daniel's chest so that he was facing Daniel. Sven's anesthesia was taking effect. Ben penned Daniel's arms to his sides by positioning his own legs outside of Daniel's arms. He was thankful he didn't have to watch Sven cut the leg. Sven, meanwhile, had positioned Daniel's good leg so that he could sit on it, holding it still with his weight. He had propped the broken leg up on a rock. The femur was broken about mid-thigh so Sven decided to take the leg off there. It would save a lot of trauma if he didn't have to break the bone again. He was very concerned about the obvious blood poisoning. Sven had tied a tourniquet above where he planned to cut to slow the loss of blood. *There are so many ways this man can die tonight and none of them are good,* Sven thought.

It's a damn bloody affair, cutting off a man's leg. Daniel almost bucked Ben completely off at one point. Ben had heard men scream, but none of them had screamed like Daniel. He finally went into shock and his body relaxed but his breathing was ragged and gasping. All three of them were

Sanctuary

THE WAHATOYA   81

soaked in blood. Sven heated his knife blade again until it glowed red. He then pressed the flat part of the blade against Daniel's stump to cauterize the blood vessels. Then he applied the resin mixture to the wound and wrapped it tightly with strips of canvas he had cut from the plane's interior. He tied it all up and gave Daniel another application of anesthesia.

naiku

He and Ben were exhausted. Sven led Ben out of the room and down a long corridor. Ben could hear a loud rushing sound, which grew louder as they walked.

"You should know about the other entrance to this cave. It'll make a good emergency exit."

The darkness in the cave was fading as they neared the source of the sound. A mottled light filled the cavern when they turned the last corner.

"I'll be damned," Ben exclaimed. "We're behind a water fall."

"The Utes called this the Cave of Falling Waters. These days most people refer to the waterfall as Chaparral Falls. No one else knows about the cave. Let's get washed off."

Ben felt much better after cleansing himself of all the blood but he dreaded going back into the room with Daniel. Sven had wrapped the amputated leg up and taken it outside to bury. Together they moved Daniel into another area of the cave, away from the bloody operating room. Ben didn't see how Daniel could possibly survive that ordeal. Ben made him as comfortable as possible under the circumstances. Sven showed Ben how to apply the anesthesia to Daniel's gums. Daniel drifted in and out of consciousness. Sven's potion was helping to keep the bleeding in check but the make shift bandage was already turning red. Ben had to wonder if the trauma and pain were worth it to simply postpone Daniel's death.

They set up camp in another room. Evidently there was a series of corridors and small rooms in this mountain complex. Sven told him how Towaoc, the great Ute chief, had brought him here when Sven was a young man.

"The Utes used the complex to store food for use in the winter. They used one of the rooms as a sweat lodge to conduct religious ceremonies. The women and children used it as a hiding place during a fierce battle with the Spanish settlers, during which time Towaoc's first child, a baby girl, my future wife, was born."

Ben looked at him. "So, you were married?"

"Yes, I was married for many years. I'm going to get us something to eat. Don't leave the cave." Sven left.

naiku

All of a sudden the silence weighed heavily on Ben. He could hear Daniel's labored breathing. He forced himself to walk into the room with him. Daniel's eyes were open and locked on Ben.

"I'm surprised to be alive," he whispered.

"You've got a tough road to travel my friend," Ben replied as he bent down on his haunches where Daniel could see his face.

"You mean die here in the dark or have the Nazis drag me back to Germany where they'll surely kill me as soon as I give them what they want?"

Ben nodded his head in agreement.

"You know, Ben. I'm a loyal American. I just couldn't let my parents die in a gas chamber. Now that I know how many people have died and think about the people who may yet die, because of my actions, I'm not sure I can justify what I've done. War is about terrible sacrifices and horrible choices, isn't it?"

Ben thought, *I know something about good men sacrificing their lives for a cause.* But he couldn't judge Daniel.

"Yes, it is and war does not discriminate when demanding sacrifice." Ben continued, "My mother used to quote the Bible in good times and in bad times. During the depression my father was injured in an accident and couldn't plow the fields for the spring planting. My mother had to look after me and get the fields plowed. Looking back on that time, I realize how desperate she must have felt. The verse that seemed to bring her the most comfort and give her hope was out of Psalms."

Ben recited from memory,

The LORD is my shepherd; I shall not want. He maketh me to lie down in green pastures: he leadeth me beside the stillwaters. He restoreth my soul: he leadeth me in the paths of righteousness for his name's sake. Yea, though I walk through the valley of the shadow of death, I will fear no evil: for thou art with me; thy rod and thy staff they comfort me. Thou preparest a table before me in the presence of mine enemies: thou anointest my head with oil; my cup runneth over. Surely goodness and mercy shall follow me all the days of my life: and I will dwell in the house of the LORD for ever.

THE WAHATOYA

Ben was normally very private about how he felt about God. His faith was very real. He just never shared it. If ever there was a time to talk to someone about faith, though, this was it. Daniel nodded.

"Sven went for food. Try to rest."

"Thanks for the reminder, Ben." Daniel squeezed Ben's hand. He drifted back into unconsciousness and Ben wiped his face and forehead with a damp cloth. Ben noticed that the dressing on Daniel's leg, no his stump, was red-soaked again. Daniel opened his eyes. "Tell me about your family, Ben. Your mother sounds like a remarkable woman."

"She was. I just wish I had known it sooner. She was really my only parent when I was growing up. My father worked all the time—every day and all day. He was always mending fence, chasing a wayward cow or bull, plowing a field, delivering a calf. He couldn't afford to hire help. My mom took care of me and the house. I heard them get into terrible arguments about my staying in school or helping with the endless tasks around the farm. My mother always won that argument. I used to feel like my father resented my going to school, so I would work extra hard on weekends and during summer vacations trying to earn his approval." Ben cradled Daniel's head with his arm and gave him some water. He drank with long gulps. "How did you get from the farm to flying airplanes?"

"Mom died when I was sixteen and my father withdrew even deeper into his lonely existence. I would get up at sunrise to help with chores, and then go to school. I guess he felt that he needed to honor Mom's passion that I finish high school so he never suggested that I stay home to help. I don't really know how we made it those last two years of high school. We didn't have any close neighbors but one of my friends would bring an extra lunch for me. When I got home each day I would work at chores until dark. It was a bleak existence. Of course I missed my mother terribly. She had been my only bright spot. My father's inattention became even more oppressive without her smile and comfort. The day after I graduated I packed my meager belongings and hitchhiked to Randolph Field in San Antonio. We got occasional news about the war and every kid I knew was signing up. One of my few forms of entertainment back then was watching the planes from Randolph Air Field practice dog-fighting in the skies above our farm. They would sometimes buzz our field, flying so low I could see the pilot's goggles. I was fascinated with the planes' power and the idea of flying above the clouds. On the day I left the farm, I stood at the end of the row my father was plowing. Our old mule was plodding straight toward me. My father struggled to keep the plow straight as the mule pulled it through the hardscrabble earth. I at least wanted to say good-by. He reached the end of the row and, without looking up, turned the mule around and started down the next row. I just stood there watching him manhandle the plow as the distance between us grew even longer. I left without ever saying or hearing good-by. I was a pretty smart kid and the Army Air Force welcomed me. They've been my family ever since."

Ben wondered if he would ever see any of his family again.

A Desperate Search

Michael gathered his meager team around him. Agent Brian King told them about the two Germans who were evidently trailing Sven. Sheriff Lonnie Dunn spoke up. "We have the advantage. I know where Sven is headed." He squatted on his haunches and began drawing in the moist dirt. "Sven is probably already in the cave behind Chaparral Falls. The entrances are so well hidden that no one could find them without help." He drew a crude map. "Here's what I think we need to do. Joe Cordova and I will head directly for Chaparral Falls. I'll set Joe up in a position where he can watch the back door and have a good view of all the approaches to the falls. I'm going to go in the back door, so to speak, through the water fall and try to find them in the cave. I'll bet Sven led the Germans in an ever tightening concentric circle to confuse them. He then more-than-likely slipped outside the circle and the Germans are probably following his old footsteps round and round. The cave is about here." Lonnie tapped the earth. "I suggest you gentlemen," nodding to Michael and Agent King, "track the Germans and try to intercept them somewhere along the circle that Sven lay down." Lonnie described the landmarks between their position and the cave and explained how to find the cave's entrance "Joe and I will exit the canyon and approach the cave from the other direction." He pointed to the spot where he planned to position Joe with his rifle. "I've gotta tell you, Joe Cordova is the best shot in the county—maybe even the best shot on the mountain today." He looked at Agent King with a twinkle in his eye and allowed himself to smile. Brian King grinned and said, "I look forward to seeing the results of your work, Sheriff Cordova."

Michael also smiled at the subtle challenge to Brian's marksmanship. *This guy is probably one of the best three or four marksmen in the world and he's always willing to acknowledge another shooter's skill. That's why men love serving with him,* he thought to himself. Sheriff Cordova smiled back at Brian and gave him an abbreviated salute, one guy trying to serve his country to another. Michael spoke up, "I like your plan. We can put them in a pincer and squeeze them. It won't take them long to figure out that Sven has slipped out of this circle, though. It would be a terrible mistake to underestimate these men." Michael looked at each man to emphasize this last comment. "Sheriff Dunn, I think you need to return to your office. The cavalry will be arriving in La Veta in a short time and they'll need your help finding us. Besides, you might be needed in town. Who knows what other surprises the Nazis have brought from the Fatherland?" Lonnie thought for a minute. "You're right. Joe knows where to go and what to do and I'll be more use to the boys from Washington when they get here."

None of them truly understood just how dangerous the two Germans were.

The Best of the Worst

The two Nazis were in the top ranks, so to speak, of Hitler's youth movement. Like most young men reaching the age of fourteen, Arndt and Dietmar moved from the Jungvolk to the Hitler Youth for indoctrination and training. They left their homes and, in essence, began their military basic training and their social indoctrination. Only a very few Americans-those in the intelligence community-had the slightest idea of the nature of the youth-to-killer transformation that was taking place in Hitler's Germany. The length and severity of the HitlerYouth's combat training surpassed anything the United States military provided its own fighting forces.

Arndt and Dietmar were roommates throughout their training and developed a close bond, almost like that of brothers. Perhaps from being yanked from their homes at such an early age. But Hitler was more interested in the military than in any social ramifications. Hitler envisioned a super soldier who would conquer the world in his name.

By the age of eighteen, Arndt and Dietmar had completed the equivalent of army Ranger training. They were both expert marksmen and skilled in hand-to-hand combat. At the completion of each training phase, the boy-soldiers were subjected to intense physical and mental evaluations. Only those who performed superbly were advanced to the next phase of training. Arndt and Dietmar consistently scored at the top of their classes, alternating between finishing number one and number two. Arndt was more cold blooded and quicker to make a tactical decision. His single-minded focus and his resolve to succeed at any cost sometimes caused even his diabolical and cruel trainers to take pause. The final training mission was designed to put the trainees in an impossible, confusing situation to evaluate how they reacted and to test their decision making skills under extreme pressure. By this time, the students were well trained, highly disciplined and had demonstrated their loyalty beyond any doubt. This last exercise was more of an experiment than a test. Arndt was dropped off in an isolated part of a forest, given a map and told that enemy combatants were hiding in a nearby house. After he entered the house, he had sixty seconds to kill them all. It seemed too simple to Arndt. The Germans often used live, expendable subjects in their training to add realism. Shooting a target was one thing. Looking into a man's eyes in the face of death was another. The house was surrounded by dense foliage so it was easy for Arndt to stay hidden until he was nearly at the front door. Arndt suspected a trick; the door was not even locked. He was dumbfounded when he entered the small house and saw his parents. The looks on their faces went from puzzlement to relief when Arndt came through the door. The training observers, who were monitoring the exercise from several vantage points, rushed into the house when they heard the gun shots. Time elapsed: thirty-four seconds.

Dietmar was the more thoughtful and calculating of the pair. He had the better strategic vision. Dietmar would sometimes take a step back if he saw that it would eventually lead to accomplishing the objective. Arndt was more apt to forge ahead with superior strength and skill even if it didn't get him closer to his goal. Arndt was slightly stronger than Dietmar but Dietmar had quicker feet and hands, which gave him a slight advantage in hand-to-hand combat. They both hated the United States. They didn't know why but they did. They were a formidable pair.

They had split up to track Sven. By now they felt a grudging admiration for their prey. He had thrown them off the trail twice now. They vowed it wouldn't happen again. Arndt was tracking while Dietmar shadowed him from cover of the dense forest—watching and listening. They never assumed that they were alone on the mountain with their target. The arrival of the search and rescue team at the crash site had told them the Americans were also after their defector. Arndt and Dietmar knew the importance of the information that Daniel was trying to get to Hitler's scientists and it would be foolish to think that the Americans would not try to intervene.

After a couple hours of tracking, Arndt could tell that the trail was leading them in circles. They split up to search for Sven's exit point. They knew that Sven was pulling a litter with someone on it and Arndt had discovered that the trailing pair of footsteps was lagging some distance behind. So, they had one too wounded to walk and another was struggling to keep up. Their prey appeared to be slowing and weakening. The unknown was where and when the other Americans would appear. They set out to find where Sven had broken the circle. He was probably hiding while he waited to be rescued.

THE WAHATOYA

89

naiku

Daniel had slipped into a restless state of semi consciousness but his breathing sounded better. Ben sat down with his back to the wall and allowed himself to drift off. He heard his mother singing softly in the kitchen. He watched the morning sun caress the distant horizon. He strained to make out the words, but could only hear her voice and the melody. It was the most cherished memory of his childhood. The feelings of absolute comfort and security came in the early mornings when his mom would gently wake him with her singing. Ben would get up and hurry into the kitchen, anxious to see his mom again and feel her warmth surround him. He must have taken a wrong turn because her voice was behind him now.

"Mom, where are you?" he cried out in a child's voice of apprehension.

"It's alright, Ben. Don't be afraid," she reassured him. He spun around and saw her standing in the kitchen doorway. She was smiling at him as she dried her weathered hands with her apron. He ran to her. That apron had dried many of Ben's tears as a young boy. It was soft and reassuring while his world was often hard and unforgiving. She dried away his tears.

The aroma of his mom's cooking turned to the acrid smoke filling his cockpit as he fought to regain control of his B-24, falling in an ever-tightening spin. He could hear the screams of his wounded crew. His hands were on the controls but he couldn't make anything happen. They kept spinning and his crew kept screaming.

"I'm trying! I'm trying!" Ben screamed as he jumped awake.

"Take it easy. Take it easy." Sven gently shook Ben awake. "That must have been one hell of a dream. But things are looking up. I brought supper." Sven held up the carcass of a rabbit. He quickly skinned and gutted the animal, then skewered the meat on a long stick and propped it over the fire. The fire popped and fizzled from the dripping grease. The space was soon filled with the aroma of cooking meat.

"Sven, what are our chances of getting out of here alive?" Ben felt remarkably better after the meager dinner. Daniel had also eaten and fallen into a fitful sleep.

"Lonnie Dunn will figure out that we should have been back by now. And if they made it to the crash site, they've discovered the bodies of the FBI agents. Lonnie's the only other person besides me who knows about this cave. We have to wait it out and hope our guys take care of the Germans and come get us." Sven lowered his voice. "Now for him," he nodded his head toward Daniel. "I don't have much hope. I probably just delayed his death by taking off his leg." Sven sat down with his back against the wall. He was exhausted. The coals of the dying fire radiated a soft glow that barely held the darkness at bay.

"Do you have any family around here, Sven?" Ben shifted his body so that he faced in Sven's direction.

"I have a son who lives on the Ute Indian Reservation in Ignacio."

"So he must be part Indian?"

"His mother was a full-blooded Ute. She was the daughter of Towaoc, the Ute chief who took me in. We practically grew up together." Sven's voice softened considerably as he drudged up those oh-so-ancient memories. "Sometimes it was pretty tough for a white kid growing up with the Indians, especially when the white man was the source of many of their problems. And of course the white families didn't know what to make of my living arrangements, but then, none of them had volunteered to take me in. No doubt about it, the Utes saved my life."

Ben sensed a change in Sven's demeanor and he could almost feel the presence of the Ute tribe.

"Her name was Shavano, which means 'Blue Flower', but Towaoc nicknamed her Lily because the Mountain Lily was his favorite flower. She resented my coming into their camp at first, but grudgingly accepted me when she realized that I was doing many of the chores. I was a pretty shy kid to begin with, and for a long time I was intimidated by the young Ute braves, so I just didn't pay much attention to her."

Telling the story began to relax Sven and he smiled as he continued. "When I was about fourteen, I went with Lily, who was probably about thirteen, and her mother, Amache, to pick berries. Amache and I were each focused on our own efforts to find the best berries, when Lily began screaming. We looked around frantically but couldn't locate her. I scrambled onto a rock outcropping just as she screamed again. I saw the top of her head as she ran through the thick bushes. I yelled at her mother, pointing in Lily's direction, taking off toward her. I found her in a small clearing, just in time to come face to face with two white boys from the settlement. They were older, and substantially bigger, than I was and were intent on mischief.

"Many of the white settlers, unlike most of the Spaniards who had settled in the area, were contemptuous of the Indians. Who knows if those two were just having a little fun or if they would have done Lily serious harm. At first glance, I didn't pose much of a threat to the bigger boys and I'm sure they counted on my running away. But when you lived with the Utes, you quickly learned to fight in order to survive. I had learned my lesson and developed

THE WAHATOYA

into a pretty formidable fighter. Most of the Ute braves had found out that picking on me was not worth the pain. I had decided that when defending myself, there was no such thing as a fair fight.

"I tore into the first intruder headfirst and caught him square in the solar plexus. I heard the air rushing from his lungs. He lay on the ground, gasping. I rolled over and jumped to my feet. The other one grabbed a stick and was waving it in my direction. We circled each other a couple of times, each of us trying to predict the other's next move. He swung the stick at my head. I ducked and rolled on the ground, grabbing a handful of dirt. As I regained my footing, I flung the dirt in his face. Before he could recover, I picked up a rock and smashed his nose. Muddy blood gushed from his nose and he dropped to his knees, screaming. He tried to clear his eyes but ended up rubbing mud and blood into them, making them even worse. I grabbed the stick he had dropped and turned to his buddy. He had recovered his footing by then and stood, waving a knife side to side. He made a few trial thrusts, which I dodged.

"By now Amache was standing in front of Lily at the edge of the clearing. The white boys couldn't have known it but if they got past me, they would face a force much like a mother bear protecting her cub. I had heard the story of how Amache almost killed Towaoc and his best friend, Quenche, after Towaoc had kidnapped Amache from her family's camp to marry her." Sven allowed a rare smile to break out.

"I faked a swing at his head and when he raised his arm in defense, I half squatted and swung my right leg behind him, sweeping his feet out from under him. He landed squarely on his back. I was on my feet quickly and swung the stick as hard as I could. I connected solidly with his collar bone. I heard it crack just before he screamed in agony. Just then a third boy appeared from nowhere. He probably had come looking for his friends and had come on the scene just in time to see me bash one of them with a large stick. He crashed into me, running at full speed. My head bounced off the hard ground and I blacked out momentarily. I regained consciousness hearing a familiar growl near my head.

'Get him off! Get him off!' screamed the boy who had just laid me low, now thrashing and terrified.

"Now I had his weight and Lobo's on top of me. Lobo had been watching patiently until he saw me in trouble. Then he turned into a snarling, chomping hound from hell. He had grown to about one-hundred-fifteen pounds by that time and his thick coat made him look even bigger. He was in this fight for the kill. I rolled my head away from Lobo's powerful jaws, scooted out from under the pile and jumped to my feet. The boy had raised his arms to protect his face and throat. Lobo shredded the flesh on both his forearms. Just as he clamped his jaws on the boy's throat, I called him off.

'Lobo, come.'

He stopped, but held his teeth tightly on the boy's throat, as if to make sure everyone knew who was the stronger. After a few agonizing seconds, Lobo released his grip and ran to my side."

"As a final insult, I took the boys' knifes away from them and kept them. We gathered up our blackberry pouches and left the boys to lick their wounds, so to speak. That day my place among the Ute tribe was established forever. Not only had I defended Amache and their chief's daughter, but I had soundly defeated white boys from the settlement as well. The Utes made great ceremony out of telling stories and they told that one many times around the camp fires. Lily saw me in a different light after that. She began to talk to me and I gradually learned to express my feelings to her." Sven hesitated and Ben thought that he was finished. But talking about Lily had opened a vein of emotional memories and Sven continued. "As Lily and I spent more and more time together, both Amache and Towaoc began to disapprove. It was one thing to have a white boy living with the tribe but, it was quite another to watch a romance between me their daughter begin to blossom. Lily and I laughed about all the headshaking and the disapproving looks. She assured her mother that there was nothing romantic between the two of us. Like all mothers since the dawn of time, Amache listened to her daughter's protests with healthy skepticism. The truth was, we had become soul mates. Then one hot summer day, we were swimming in one of our secret hide-a-ways. We got out of the water and were enjoying the feel of the warm breeze." Ben looked up and saw Sven gazing at a distant time. "Something just came over me. It was like all the love I had lost when my sister, Becky, died. Plus the love my mother had for my father and his love that I never knew, came pouring into me. I felt all that love for Lily. I broke down and cried as I tried to explain all of that to her. I wasn't even speaking coherently by then but she understood all of it. I knew then that I wanted to spend the rest of my life with her. I asked her to marry me. We both broke down and cried then. By the time we had collected ourselves and started back to the camp, the specter of Towaoc and Amache loomed very large in our thoughts."

Sven was on a roll. He told about asking old Saí-ar for her advice. The old surrogate grandmother was almost totally blind but she still had all her wits about her. She told Sven the story about when Towaoc was a young chief, he had become so enamored with Amache, that he spent two days hiding

Confrontation

in the brush around her camp watching and plotting so that he could steal her away. He had enlisted the help of his most trusted friend and warrior, Quenche. In the dark of night, Towaoc thundered into Amache's camp on his famous black horse and swept her off the ground. Quenche was waiting for him and helped divert the pursuing braves. When they stopped to check on their captive princess, she turned into a kicking, slashing devil, almost slicing Towaoc's belly open with her knife. Quenche had to hit her on the head to save his and Towaoc's lives. Saí-ar laughed loudly and rocked back and forth as she told the story.

Saí-ar continued, "Young Amache lived in my tepee. She swore that she would never marry a man who would kidnap her and dishonor her father, who was also a chief. Towaoc had made a serious blunder but he came up with a plan to make it right. He agreed to return Amache to her camp if she still wanted to leave after living in our camp for two weeks. During that time, she learned much about Towaoc and those who loved him. After her anger left, she decided to stay. Towaoc made the proper arrangements and rode into her father's camp wearing a beautiful white headdress to honor the occasion. He rode on his magnificent black horse with many of his braves riding by his side. Then he honored Amache's father and their entire camp with a gift of many horses." She smiled and whispered, "It was believed by many, that the kidnapping took place with her father's unspoken approval. You see, an unmarried daughter causes a father, especially one who is also the chief, much more grief than marrying her off to a different tribe."

She told Sven that he had to demonstrate to Towaoc and to the camp that he was worthy of marrying the chief's daughter. He had to show Towaoc much respect and honor Towaoc's feelings in the matter. "Forget about being a white boy who wants to marry an Indian girl. Show the tribe that you're a man with dignity and honor who wants to marry the one he loves." Saí-ar patted his hand.

Sven thought for many days about what Saí-ar had told him. He wanted to be a man of honor and he wanted the camp's respect but most of all he wanted Lily to be proud of him. He needed a worthy gesture.

Sven visited Father Miguel, whom he found in the Spanish settlement, splitting firewood.

"Sven, it's good to see you." As usual, the priest gave Sven a warm hug and made him feel like he had been waiting all day just to see him. Much like he had done with the young orphan, Towaoc, Miguel had provided a safe haven for Sven after his mother left. The priest had introduced Sven to

Telling on Towaoc

God and showed him that there was always hope, no matter how bleak and dark things appeared. Old Saí-ar had told Sven about how Father Miguel traded an old, lame horse for the young, broken orphan who grew up to be the Ute's great chief. Miguel and Saí-ar had jointly raised Towaoc and later he performed Towaoc's and Amache's wedding. She told Sven that Miguel had risked his own life after the bloody battle between the Spaniards and Utes, following the death of Sven's father and a Ute brave. Miguel had ridden into the Ute camp when emotions were at a fever pitch. He had tried to re-gain the peace they all enjoyed for so many years.

"He stood in the middle of a hundred bloodthirsty, yelping braves and talked to Towaoc and the Ute camp for hours. Nobody could question his courage or his willingness to give his own life, if necessary, to avoid more killing." Saí-ar believed that Sven and Father Miguel and her tribe had been joined together by the death of Sven's father, and that Sven had the chance and an obligation to turn that bloody tragedy into something good for all of them.

Miguel had also explained to Sven how Sven's father was killed. But he could never explain why a loving God would allow an innocent man to die in such a meaningless way. Where was God's compassion in that? The best that the priest could do was to admit that he didn't understand that either.

"We don't know the true nature of God but that's why it's called faith. Without the uncertainty, the fear, there would be no faith." The priest's sincerity and compassion for him always comforted Sven but he still struggled to understand God's place in his life.

"Don't worry, Sven. All of us struggle with that question," Father Miguel told him reassuringly. He also told Sven that he wanted him to go on a trip. He told him to climb the tallest peak of the Wahatoya and to be there in time for the sunrise.

"Let the first light of the day shine on your face and spend the rest of the day looking and thinking and feeling."

It sounded like a useless exercise to Sven, but he admired and respected Father Miguel. He and Lobo set out late one afternoon and climbed the western peak of the Wahatoya. They spent the night on the summit. Sven was amazed at the solitude and the silence—no forest noises, no rushing river, no sounds at all. He awoke just as the darkness was beginning to lose its grip on the eastern horizon. The brilliance of the awakening sky mesmerized him. For a brief moment, the layer of orange lingered as the dazzling blue burst across the heavens, as if to make sure that the new morning had things under control. Sven savored the morning warmth on his face. He and Lobo

THE WAHATOYA 97

ate their meager breakfast in silence. They spent most of the day there. Sven became very contemplative about the world and his place in it. Some people might have called his experience meditative and some might have called it religious. Sven didn't try to label it. If pressed to describe his mountain top excursion, he probably would have called it his Listening Time. If someone had pressed him further with, "Listening for what?" He probably would have said, "I don't know, just listening."

Miguel was delighted to hear about Sven and Lily and counseled Sven to be prepared for the settlers' reactions, which they both knew would not be favorable.

"The Utes will accept the marriage. But you must pay close attention to their customs and to Towaoc's position as the father and chief. Honoring him will go a long way with the tribe." Sven asked Miguel to perform the marriage ceremony.

"I would be honored," Miguel assured him.

Miguel took great pride in Sven's attention to the tribe's and Towaoc's feelings. Miguel allowed himself a moment of satisfaction for his role in raising the young run-away. Memories of Towaoc, when he rode into the settlement many years ago, flooded Miguel's mind. The Apache lad had been kidnapped by a Ute raiding party after they had killed the boy's parents. Towaoc was a warrior even then and attacked one of the Utes. They broke his leg and allowed him to live in hopes of trading him for a horse. Father Miguel knew the young captive would be killed if they couldn't trade him, so Miguel had scrounged an old lame mare from the settlement's stock. With help from Sai-r, who was already old in those days, Miguel cared for, tutored, and most importantly, loved the orphan.

Even though Miguel was the priest and the spiritual leader of the Spanish settlers, he had learned much from Towaoc and Sai-ar about spirituality. The Church would probably have considered Father Miguel a failure. After all, he did not try to convert the "savages". He tried to harmonize his God with the Great Spirit. Miguel came to believe that the differences lay not in the Spaniards' and the Indians' God, but in how God's children related to him and wove him into each of their lives. An outside observer might have labeled Miguel a "practical priest". He helped his flock clear brush, cut firewood, erect their shelters, and doctor their wounds. He mediated their differences and hunted game. First he helped them survive and then he filled their souls with the spirit of God.

It was Sai-ar who first brought Sven to the priest's attention. She was wise enough to give the boy, if he survived, a chance to grow up with the Spaniards and learn their ways. It would be much easier for him to transition into the white man's world some day if he had the advantage of the priest's influence. Miguel was a natural nurturer and teacher. He had insisted that Sven attend the settlement's school with the other children. Much like Towaoc had done, Sven divided his time between the Ute camp and the Spanish settlement. Miguel became a father figure to Sven and tried to convince him to stay in the settlement permanently. Sven was drawn to the Ute camp, though, and embraced the simplicity and the freedom of their daily lives. He loved the outdoors and how the Indians seemed part of nature, unlike the Spaniards and the white settlers, who seemed to struggle against nature.

Sven looked around the settlement as he headed back to the Indian camp. *Where did they all come from?* He wondered. Log cabins had replaced many of the sod huts and there were too many of them to count. The growing settlement stood in stark contrast to the slowly diminishing Indian camp.

naiku

He had many chores to finish at the camp, among which was to lead the tribe's horses to water. They were a mangy, docile lot and they shuffled along behind Sven on their way to the river. Sven loved them nonetheless. He paid attention to each one of them, slipping them all slices from the apples he had gotten from Father Miguel. The horses were a sad reflection of the tribe's physical and emotional decline. Then the idea hit him like a thunder bolt. *That's it. Of course!* He knew how to win Towaoc's absolute approval for his marriage to Lily. Horses.

naiku

Towaoc had earned his place as a warrior when he was sixteen years old. He had accompanied a raiding party to steal horses from a Spanish wagon train. His quick thinking and gutsy leadership saved the small band of braves from being discovered and resulted in their bringing home a herd of valuable Spanish horses. He would bring Towaoc a dowry of beautiful horses to replenish the tribe's dwindling herd. Not only would it honor Towaoc, but it would provide a rich treasure that the tribe could trade to the settlers. It was perfect. Of course, like all perfect plans, this one was full of thorny questions. Where could he find such a treasure? Was he prepared to steal that many horses? How many braves would he need to help? Then he remembered hearing a story from one of the settlers about a herd of wild horses that roamed

THE WAHATOYA   99

between the Wahatoya peaks. Many had seen the herd, which supposedly numbered between two and three hundred horses. Their leader was reportedly a fiery Mustang stallion who was fast on the run and ferocious when defending his turf. He began planning the unlikely raid in earnest and brought his two best friends into the preparations, swearing them to secrecy.

naiku

They designated a large, flat meadow, not far from the camp as the wild horses' new home. There was plenty of room and with some hard work, well placed rope and fallen Aspen trees they built a corral with a long, wide entrance. Sven then worked a deal with Father Miguel, who helped them secure three fast horses from the settlement herd. The boys would cut and carry firewood in exchange for the use of the horses.

After three weeks of planning, gathering ropes and food and preparing the corral, Sven told Lily that he would be gone for several days but when he returned, their future would be changed forever. Lily's heart raced as she listened to Sven's bravado and imagined what on earth he was planning for them.

naiku

Sven had learned a lot about horses while living with the Utes. He had ridden the big, strong Spanish horses as well as the smaller, faster Mustangs. He had broken wild horses for the Spaniards. Father Miguel had taught him how to treat many of the common ailments of frontier horses. He loved their strength and grace.

naiku

The young adventurers spent the first two days watching the Mustang herd from afar, learning their patterns. On the third day Sven took them down closer to let the Mustang stallion see them and catch the scent of them and their horses. As expected, the stallion bolted and the herd thundered after him. There were easily a hundred horses in the herd. For the first time, Sven got a close, though quick, look at the stallion. He was a magnificent animal—coal black, with a shock of white in the middle of his forehead. He was considerably bigger than the typical Mustang. Sven thought that he might be the offspring of one of the Spanish horses that got loose and mingled with the Mustang herd. What a combination of size, strength, speed and stamina! For the next three days, the young riders stayed close to the herd and rode among them when they bolted and ran. Sven tried to ride close to the stallion, but he was too fast for his horse to run with for very long. A long meadow meandered between the two peaks, then widened into a flat plain. That's where Sven wanted to direct the herd. He and the braves would have to be very careful and ride like crazy when they put his plan into motion.

Sven explained his plan and showed both of his companions where he wanted them to be when they started the stampede. He would be waiting, hidden from view, so that he could intercept the stallion on the run. His horse could run with the stallion for only a short time, so Sven wouldn't be able to chase him down. Sven and his horse hid about fifteen yards from the desired stampede path. He waved a white cloth when he was ready. The Ute riders, one on each side of the Mustang herd, began shouting and riding toward the Mustangs. The stallion reared on his hind legs, pawing the air and neighing. Sven could hear the thunder of hoofs as the herd built speed and barreled toward his position. *So far, so good.* The earth shook beneath his horse, who became fidgety and restless.

"Soon my warrior, soon and you can run to your heart's desire, Sven soothed him." He turned his excited, dancing horse to face the same direction that the herd was moving and looked over his right shoulder.

"Now!" he yelled and jabbed his heels into the horse's sides. The stallion was bearing down on them. His horse dug in and leapt into a full gallop. The stallion was gaining. Sven had to have perfect timing or his friends would be carrying his crumpled and crushed body back to Lily. Sven urged his horse forward. He needed his horse to be running neck and neck with the stallion for a couple of minutes, at least. Lobo took off also. His ancestors had been swift hunters. They had chased game across plains and through forests for generations. Lobo's pack instinct led him to a position on the opposite side of the wild, stampeding stallion. The horse was boxed in. The three of them thundered across the earth in a straight line. Sven gauged their distance and positions. Now! Sven's excited horse was at full gallop and the stallion was running in perfect unison with him. Sven eased closer, then closer to the stallion, who was running in perfect rhythm. Sven jumped. If he didn't land perfectly, it would end in a terrible death. But his legs straddled the black beauty perfectly and he grabbed a handful of flying mane. The Mustang exploded. He ran away from Sven's horse, which was already slowing. Sven braced himself and tightened his grip. His legs were snug against the Mustang's heaving sides. He knew that he was in for the ride of his life. Lobo veered away also. The chase had been successful.

THE WAHATOYA

When Sven had explained his plan to "kidnap" the Mustang herd, his friends thought he was crazy. Sven knew that the three of them couldn't hope to capture more than three or four horses and herd them back to camp. Besides, he had a grander vision. He knew that if he controlled the stallion, he could control the entire herd. He didn't like the idea of "breaking" a wild horse so it could be ridden. He preferred to bond with the horse. The wild stallion would be his greatest challenge.

naiku

The stallion turned back into the herd and began bucking. The herd slowed and began milling about while their leader careened and crashed through them. Sven's helpers found shade and dismounted. They knew it would be a long process. Sven's rider less horse found his way back and joined the small audience. The black demon bucked like a banshee for an hour. Then he pranced through the herd, scattering horses in all directions. Sven didn't budge. Finally the stallion stopped, his sides heaving as he gasped for air. Sven wasn't convinced. He held his position on the horse's back. Sure enough, the stallion exploded again, jumping straight up and twisting his body. He hit on all fours and bucked for another thirty minutes. For the rest of the day, the mighty Mustang alternated between bucking, running headlong through the scattering herd and standing stone still with his sides heaving. By dusk, Sven was wondering if he had bitten off more than he could chew. Sven was exhausted. His thighs were aching. He was dehydrated. Just before dark the stallion stopped once again but, instead of standing motionless with his withers trembling, he walked toward a stand of Aspen trees that surrounded a small creek. *I've got him,* Sven thought hopefully. Regardless, he had to get off the horse. If the horse bolted, so be it. Sven couldn't ride one minute longer. He eased his right leg over the sweaty haunches and lowered himself to the ground. His legs collapsed and he fell. Bracing himself for a whirlwind of legs and hooves, he prepared to roll away. But the exhausted stallion simply stood there, as if waiting for instructions. Sven rose and steadied himself as he shared the big horse's relief to be done. He wobbled next to the stallion and slowly moved his hand under the horse's jaw. He gently placed his fingertips against the underside of his mouth and began walking the horse toward the creek. The stallion walked beside him. They both drank from the cool mountain stream. Lobo had approached but was keeping his distance. Sven extended his arm toward Lobo and made a slow patting gesture with his hand. Lobo lowered himself to his belly and inched along the ground so as not to alarm the new member of the family. Sven pulled several handfuls of lush green grass and fed them to the horse, the whole time speaking to him in soft, measured tones.

"I'll be your best friend and I'll never forsake you," he promised.

The three Ute braves rested that night. Sven stayed close to the stallion, dozing fitfully and occasionally talking to his new friend. He watched Lobo sleep. His powerful body stretched out, huge paws twitching, upper lip quivering.

naiku

Lobo was running through the forest under a full moon. The forest was uncommonly quiet and the big wolf never tired. His legs seemed to gain strength the longer he ran. Other creatures slipped out of the moonlit shadows and joined his silent stride. The moon light glinted off their eyes and they surrounded him. Their bodies were haggard and scruffy, in stark contrast to Lobo's sleek coat and muscular frame. Together they ran like ghosts over the forest floor. A bull elk appeared out of nowhere. He was running for his life but, like the wolf pack, he moved silently under the moon. Lobo was the fastest and the strongest one of the pack. He saw his moment. He jumped with all his might and his powerful jaws closed on the elk's throat.

"Lobo, wake up boy." Sven gently prodded Lobo's flank with his foot. The wolf jumped, raised his head slightly and then went back to sleep, this time without the dreams.

Sven sent one of his riders ahead to bring Towaoc, Amache and Lily to the newly built mountain corral near the Ute camp. He wanted to make a grand entrance. Of course the excitement spread through the entire camp and all of them were on hand for Sven's arrival. Some were skeptical. Some were hopeful that Sven could win over Towaoc and be permitted to marry Lily. In any event, it was a welcome diversion from their daily chores. Sven rode the magnificent black stallion and led the massive herd into their new home. The camp spectators felt the horses' thunder beneath their feet before they heard it. Transfixed, they waited; they weren't disappointed. Sven led almost a hundred wild mustangs into the meadow-corral at a subdued gallop. Towaoc was awestruck. *How did he do this?* was his only thought. The sight of the splendid black Mustang reminded him of his own black beauty, Negro Vienti (Black Wind), of his youth. The sheer numbers of the horses still trotting into the meadow was astonishing to him and the tribe. The stallion had regained

Getting to Know You

his vigor and Sven pranced him toward the spot where Lily and her mother stood. Lily was holding her hands to her face in amazement. Tears streaked down her cheeks. She was sobbing with joy. She looked at her father, who was standing, proud before his tribe, who had suffered more than they had triumphed in the last few years. Sven rode over and extended his arm to Lily. Even though the Mustang was skittish, Sven felt comfortable and in control. Lily grabbed his hand and arm. Sven pulled her up and onto the horse's back. She wrapped her arms around his waist as he rode in a circle for all the camp to see. Amache was also in tears. Not only had Sven swept away all their objections to their marriage, he had also publicly proclaimed his love for Lily and honored her father, the Ute's beloved chief. For a brief, magical moment on their sacred mountain, the Ute Indians reveled in the memory of their past glory and grandeur.

naiku

Sven asked Towaoc for Lily's hand. Towaoc gave his blessing and asked Sven if he would care for the stallion that Sven had captured. Allowing Sven to keep the majestic stallion was Towaoc's way of publicly recognizing Sven's grand gesture.

Sven sighed and went silent for a few minutes. Sharing his past had unleashed a river of emotions. *Must be getting old*, he thought. *Maybe I'm closer to the end than I care to admit, either by those crazy Nazis or simply old age.*

"By the time our son was born, the Utes were under increasing pressure from the Spanish and American settlers moving into the Cuchara Valley. Towaoc, unlike some other Ute chiefs, recognized that driving the white man away was impossible. Their numbers were too great. He spent the last years of his life trying to hold his band together, finding new hunting grounds, trying to appease the white settlers while maintaining his tribe's dignity and mourning their eventual demise. Not only were the white settlements growing yearly, but the United States Army actually built a fort right smack in the middle of the Ute's territory. Camp Stevens turned out to be temporary but the introduction of soldiers sent a shockwave through the Ute camp."

Ben was fascinated. He realized that his own difficult childhood paled in comparison to Sven's life with the Indians. Although his living conditions had been bleak he never lacked for food and he always had a roof over his head.

Sven continued. "Towaoc's band was decimated by degrees. Their winter hunting grounds became less and less bountiful. Their summers in the Cuchara

Valley were characterized by physical and verbal confrontations, meager hunting and, worst of all, suffering from the White Mans' diseases. Father Miguel tried his best to minister, both physically and spiritually, to them but it was a lost cause. Many of the Utes died from the measles and other diseases. Many of Towaoc's band relocated to the Ute Indian Reservation in Ignacio. I couldn't bear to stay and watch the band fall apart. And I needed to keep my family alive so I moved Lily and our son to my family's old house. Lily's younger brother moved to the reservation. We never saw him again, but heard that he married and had children of his own. Towaoc and a few of the older Utes stubbornly remained at the camp. Lily and I were with him when he died. He was proud and dignified, even on his death bed. All he asked of us was to remember him with respect and to instill in our son the memories and honor of the Ute Indians. We buried him in one of these caves. He was the last of the Utes to die on this mountain."

Sven was lost in other memories that he couldn't share: how hard it was for Lily being an Indian in a white man's world, how they both struggled to raise their son, Steven, in that white world, while trying to honor and teach him about his heritage.

Lily was saddened by the move from her beloved camp. She missed seeing her mother and father every day. Sven eventually built a tepee for him and Lily not far from the family house. Lily just could not sleep in the confining atmosphere of a permanent structure. She missed the open fire and the crackling embers by her bed. Whether it was an unconscious act of rebellion against moving, or just a terrible case of homesickness, didn't matter. She was unhappy and Sven wanted to please her. Lily would visit the camp often. She loved Sven and knew that he was trying to please her but she was trapped between the white world and the Indian world. They rarely went into the settlement and didn't have any settler friends.

The birth of their child proved to be a turning point for both Sven and Lily. Lily reveled in her new role in life and took great pleasure in taking her new son to visit his grandparents at the Indian camp. Towaoc was completely smitten with the baby and would carry him around to all of the tepees as if no one had seen him yet. As Steven grew, he displayed many attributes of his Ute grandfather. He was fearless. He loved the outdoors, and often explored the mountain. Sven took him to Chaparral Falls and showed him the hidden entrances. Through the years, Sven shared more and more about what the cave meant and its secrets, including the gold coins and how they came to be there. During his pre-teen and teenage years, Steven was more Indian than white. He identified with the stories about Towaoc and the Utes. Despite this, he got along well with the white kids at the settlement school. He was very likeable and his personality drew kids and adults alike to him. His quick mind and a sharp wit became his best defenses against the occasional insult about his heritage. He could out talk and out charm even the most strident verbal bully. Woe to those who didn't accept his good-natured witticisms and move along. When a particularly obnoxious new kid decided to "give the half-breed a good ass-kicking," Steven didn't waste his time placating him. When it was really time to fight, why waste time talking? If a fighting gene existed, Steven had it. He broke the new kid's nose with an explosive first blow. Then Steven hauled him to his feet before he could regain his senses and broke two of his ribs with quick, hard punches. By now the dazed bully was completely out of air. His nose was gushing blood and he couldn't inhale through his mouth without excruciating pain from his ribs. Steven stood there watching him impassively.

"Are you ready to apologize?" he asked.

The kid gurgled something, but only bloody bubbles came from his mouth. Steven stepped toward him.

"I want to hear your apology, now."

The kid finally caught a breath.

"I aapwagize. I'm swawy." The kid was crying now and holding up his hands in a feeble defensive gesture. Steven walked away.

Even though he was a good student, Steven lost his appetite for school when he was sixteen. He grew impatient with the boring lessons. He broke the news to Sven and Lily.

"I want to go to the reservation and meet my uncle and live with the Indians for awhile."

Lily was heartbroken. She couldn't bear to lose Steven even though she loved the idea of his wanting to live his heritage instead of just hearing about it. She cried for days after he left. Sven accepted it quite stoically but he missed Steven terribly and worried about his wellbeing. He had visited the reservation in Ignacio and was horrified at the Indians' living conditions.

"Sorry, I got lost in some very old memories." Sven confessed to Ben. "Lily passed away several years ago. She lived long enough to see Steven get married to a beautiful Indian girl from Durango. They have two children and I get to see them often."

"That's quite a story, Sven." Ben told him with admiration. "What about Lobo?"

"Lobo became more and more restless. Sometimes I noticed him staring into the forest and if I listened closely, I could hear a distant wolf howl. He

THE WAHATOYA

was listening to a faraway wolf pack. Once in a while, he would answer with a long, mournful howl. He was growing anxious, unsettled. One day we went on a long trek into the forest, going deeper into the woods than I had ever been before. On the third night of the trip, after the campfire had died down, Lobo went on full alert. He lowered his ears and growled deep in his throat. I heard movement nearby. Then I saw the glowing eyes, piercing the darkness. My heart jumped into my throat, not out of fear, but out of sorrow because I knew that I was about to lose Lobo forever.

'It's time Lobo. You need to go,' I whispered, rubbing his head. He hesitated, then bolted into the dark forest to his new family. I was elated for his freedom but my heart broke. I stayed there for two more days and nights. I don't know why, maybe hoping he would come back, maybe hoping to catch a glimpse of him again, but he was gone." Sven stared into the fire. Ben honored his memories with silence.

Ben wondered if Towaoc's and Lobo's spirits wandered among the mountain and forest watching over Sven. Little did he know that before it was over, they were going to need all the help they could get.

Call of the Wild

Lobo

Seven wolves had wandered from their usual hunting grounds, drawn close by Lobo's scent. They showed themselves despite their fear of the human. Once Lobo joined them, the motley pack broke into a run, anxious to put distance between them and the human.

Lobo was increasingly dreaming of other wolves. He formed a close bond with the human, but his ancestors' calls to the forest had prevailed. He ran easily, in stride with the fleeing wolves, euphoric with a new freedom. They took him deeper into Wahatoya's thick, dark forest—where humans dared not venture. Other wolves joined them until the entire pack had congregated into a growling horde. These wolves were more an assortment of scraggly, ill-tempered ruffians than they were a pack. There was no alpha male or alpha female to keep control, lead the hunts, and ensure that only the strongest wolves reproduced. Alarmed by the human scent, which was still strong on Lobo, several of the males circled him and snapped at his flanks. None of them confronted him face-to-face. Lobo's instinct reared its ferocious head and he tore into the two closest males. The darkness was filled with the sounds of battle—snarling, growling and yelps of pain. Two of the wolves lay dead, one with his throat torn open, the other with a crushed skull. Other males, excited by the smell of blood, attacked the stranger. But Lobo was bigger and stronger and he had the heart of a warrior. After two more males lay dead and another limped into the dark undergrowth to lick his wounds, Lobo stood alone. His eyes gleamed with the excitement of the kill, his exposed teeth shining in the moonlight. He glared at the wolves, challenging them with a harsh, guttural sound. The wolves slowly slinked away, averting their gazes. All but one female. She stood her ground, snarling and exposing her teeth. He approached her, growling, their noses almost touching. With hackles raised and ears flattened, Lobo tensed his body, preparing to tear into the female. Then the female lowered her gaze, almost imperceptibly, and Lobo relaxed. He had found his alpha female. She stood her ground in the face of certain death but then had yielded to his dominance. The smells of blood and fighting overwhelmed the human scent and the female no longer feared Lobo.

They soon mated, and began their lifelong union. Their pairing would anchor the largest and most powerful wolf pack in the woodland of the Wahatoya. Lobo raised his head to the starry sky. His soulful howl reverberated through the moonlit darkness. It woke the creatures of the day and sent shivers through the creatures of the night. Sven awakened with a start and sat upright in his sleeping bag. Lobo's howl floated on the moonlight and pierced Sven's heart.

May the Great Spirit run with you, my friend.

Deadly Reunion

Joe Cordova settled into his nest to wait and watch. He had made sure that he couldn't be spotted from any direction, but could see in every direction except directly behind him. There was a rock wall there so no one could sneak up behind him. Joe was not a trained sniper like Brian King but he had been hunting on and around these mountains all his life. Before he was old enough to shoot, he had tramped along beside his father, watching and learning the fundamentals and the nuances of hunting. Shooting game was the easy part. The tracking, the patience and the waiting were the real skills, whether hunting elk or man. Joe had served as Game Warden for twenty years before becoming Sheriff. He knew every game trail in and around the Wahatoya. He had tracked man and beast in every kind of weather. Over the years, the myth had outgrown the man, but Joe realized that was to his advantage and he didn't try too hard to dispel the myth. True, he was a deadly marksman and yes, he was a pretty good hand-to-hand fighter. Poachers were often desperate and sometimes lashed out without thinking of the consequences. Joe's prowess with a hunting knife became well-known and was often the most wildly exaggerated of his skills. Supposedly, Joe's knife was just as swift and deadly thrown with either his right or his left hand, usually under-handed. According to the legend, he always threw for the jugular vein. If the jugular was torn open, the target had only minutes to live. If they didn't choke on their own blood they bled to death. Joe often joked about some of the stories he heard about himself, but only around his closest friends. He often found himself, without backup, tracking poachers well after dark. Many time he had walked out of the darkness, into the light of a desolate campfire to interrupt a beer-soaked brag-fest. In the fraction of a second after he announced, "My name's Joe Cordova and I'm the game warden", he wanted all the testicles at that campsite to jump right up against every adams apple. The surprise, the fear and the mental image of a punctured jugular gave him the advantage, even when he was outmanned

112

GARY L. BRIDGES

and outgunned. Hopefully, he wouldn't have to get that close to these Nazis. They may not have heard all the stories about him.

naiku

Arndt sat down, disgusted. He lost the Americans again. Arndt had never lost a trail and Sven had outsmarted him three times. Dietmar stayed hidden and continued to visually sweep the landscape surrounding their position. He really didn't want to be near Arndt when he was like this. There was no telling how he might lash out. The two men were evenly matched in physical strength and fighting skill but Arndt had an explosive viciousness that was impossible to defend against.

Arndt heard a rustle and saw movement about a hundred feet away. He hunkered down behind a rock outcropping and swung up his weapon. A large, black head emerged from the shrubs and Arndt watched as the black bear waddled out into the open. She stood about four feet tall at the shoulders and must have weighed three-hundred pounds. Then, to his surprise, two black fuzz balls toddled out behind her. One of the cubs latched his teeth onto his sibling's ear and they rolled into a baby-groveling ball of fur. Every human being on earth smiles at the sight of brand new baby bear cubs playing. Every one except Arndt, that is. He ignored the cubs and stared at the mama bear. She had stood up on her hind legs and was easily six feet tall or more. But Arndt was really interested in her nose. Black bears have terrible eye sight but are blessed with keen ears and a supersensitive sense of smell. The bear was standing and sniffing to better capture a faint scent she had detected on the evening breeze. After a few seconds of scent reconnaissance, she dropped to all fours and shuffled off with a determined gait. Arndt followed, keeping downwind and low to the ground. What scent would grab a bear's attention on a normally deserted mountain side? Maybe it was a scent created by man. It wasn't much but Arndt was ready for any straw to grasp. Dietmar had also seen the bear and shadowed Arndt. After about an hour, the bear stopped. She stood again and tested the air, apparently searching for the elusive odor. All of a sudden, she dropped to all fours, whirled around and expelled a loud *wuff-wuff* to her cubs. They stopped playing and scurried to the nearest tree. Black bear cubs are born climbers. Within seconds they were sitting on a high tree limb, looking down for their mama. She was hiding in a stand of thorny bushes. She growled a muted *wuff* to the cubs, apparently telling them to sit tight. If someone or something cornered or surprised her with her cubs, the black bear sow would turn into a furry buzz saw. If a blow from her paw

THE WAHATOYA

didn't break your neck, her claws would slice you open from end to end. But given the time and space, she prefers to send her cubs to safety and avoid a fight. Fighting can cause injury and with very young cubs to look after, the mama prefers diplomacy.

Very interesting. I wonder what she smelled or heard that scared her? Arndt thought. The bear had indeed caught the man scent and she was hard wired to avoid man if at all possible

They were losing daylight fast. Arndt made his way to the bear's last position and looked around. He was standing on a large rock outcropping about fifty feet in diameter, with a steep drop-off at the southern end. He surveyed the site: no way to see tracks, no visible openings or disturbances. Arndt was oblivious that he stood just feet from the entrance to Daniel's hiding place. Darkness fell with a vengeance. Arndt felt invisible in the blackness and stood up to stretch his cramped legs.

Joe Cordova took one last look around as darkness surrounded him. All of a sudden, a full moon rose above West Peak. The giant orange sphere bathed the mountainside in an eerie light. Joe looked toward the moon. "Holy shit." Arndt was there, standing straight up, illuminated by the giant, shining ball. Joe drew up his rifle and peered through the scope. He could tell from the body shape and the posture that it wasn't either of the American agents. It wouldn't be Sven because Sven never carried a rifle; this man had one slung over his shoulder. He had to decide now whether or not to shoot. The target wouldn't last more than a few seconds once he realized he was lit up like a carnival ride.

BAM! The gunshot split the still night air like a cannon and echoed up and down the mountain.

Arndt heard the shot just as he was slammed hard to the rock surface. The bullet ripped through his shoulder. He was unconscious before he hit the ground.

"Damn." Joe exclaimed. *Now what have I done? I can't find him in the dark and I don't know how close his buddy is. Shit.* He chastised himself for having an itchy trigger finger but then consoled himself for eliminating one of the bad guys.

Michael and Agent King also heard the shot. They waited, still and tense, for a moment. Silence returned to the mountain. There were no other shots. That told Michael and Brian that there was no gun fight.

Brian whispered, "That was a thirty-ought-six, Joe Cordova's rifle. If he was in position where Lonnie said he would be by now, the Nazis must have gotten close to Sven's hiding place."

Mama Bear and Cubs

THE WAHATOYA   115

Michael nodded. There was no way to know if Joe had hit his target or, if it was a fatal shot. He knew that neither was reckless with their shooting so Joe must have felt he had a good shot. He knew that the Germans would have split up, with one of them hidden and watching.

He's in the same dilemma we are, not knowing if his comrade is dead or wounded or just hiding. If we go blundering about in the dark, though, he's got the advantage because he knows his partner's last location and will set up an ambush position near by. Michael pondered their options; wait for daylight or start making their way toward Sven's hideout.

Dietmar didn't panic. He never panicked. Less than a heartbeat after he watched Arndt knocked to the ground, he heard the gun shot. *Was Arndt alive or dead?* Dietmar remained still even though the darkness had swallowed him. Movement meant noise—the rustle of leaves, the snap of a twig. He would wait—and watch.

Michael knew that the Germans were some distance away. He had memorized the map that Lonnie had drawn for him and knew from the nearby landmarks that they were about a mile from the cave's upper entrance. So there was no risk of being overheard in their current position.

The moon gave Michael just enough light to draw in the dirt. "Okay, we know that Joe Cordova is somewhere here, watching the back entrance at the waterfall. If the Germans were snooping or getting close to the other entrance, which is about here, then Joe's shot would have traveled from here to about here." Michael dug his primitive drawing tool into the ground. "Given the direction, we know where they were traveling from after they climbed out of the canyon. With the topography immediately around the cave's upper entrance, they would have to approach it from within this arc." He drew a curved line. "Agreed?" Agent King nodded. "The dead or wounded one is probably in this area and his partner most likely stayed concealed, waiting for the shooter to show himself." *If his partner is wounded too badly to move himself or is dead, he better serves as bait for the shooter. If he is able to move himself, both he and his partner can stay concealed, which allows them to maintain that advantage.*" Brian looked at Michael.

"We need to flush this one out." Michael nodded.

"Just what I was thinking."

naiku

Michael usually did his best thinking and scheming when under extreme pressure. He knew that the Germans were experts. He knew about the Hitler

Youth and their absolute fanaticism. He had to come up with something totally unexpected. Something that the Nazis had not practiced for since they were fourteen years old. He needed a surrogate, something or someone to force the hiding Nazi out in the open.

An idea began to blossom. It was audacious and reckless and it embodied the scariest law in all of nature—the law of unintended consequences. Michael told Agent King his plan.

"I like it," Brian responded. They slept for a few hours and waited for dawn. As soon as they had enough light to see, Michael took off on a roundabout trek to position himself for the start of his grand plan (or folly, depending on the way the wind blew). Brian King climbed a giant Ponderosa pine tree and settled into a comfortable shooting position. He could see the surrounding terrain. Having a plan and moving on it had invigorated him. Now it was all up to Michael to flush out the enemy.

Michael moved quickly toward his target area. He knew that he was sacrificing stealth for speed but it was imperative that he get into the best position possible to set his plan into motion. He recalled looking at the wall map in Sheriff Dunn's office when Lonnie had first briefed the search team on the most likely position of the B-24 crash. After the briefing, Lonnie had confided in Michael that he was very concerned about fire danger in the area and hoped that the crash had not ignited a forest fire.

"Even though we've had a lot of snow on the mountain, there's a tremendous amount of standing dead trees and the forest floor is covered with dead trees. Some of them have been drying out for years. Those conditions, combined with the lack of humidity, make for a dangerous environment. A lightning strike or a wayward spark could set off a wild lands fire."

Michael was glad that he didn't have to explain his plan to Sheriff Dunn. That would have to wait. He remembered a long ago session of outdoor survival training early in his career. The instructor was explaining how to survive (or better yet, escape) a forest fire:

"Remember, fire burns faster and hotter uphill so plan your escape route accordingly."

When on outdoor, clandestine operations Michael, like all good agents, was keenly aware of the environmental conditions. He had made mental notes about the direction of the wind ever since they first entered the canyon and began tracking the Germans. He factored that into deciding on ground zero. By the time he reached his destination, he was breathing heavily from the exertion but he had no time to waste. He picked a stack of dead Aspen trees and rearranged a few of them so that the air could move more easily through the pile to feed

THE WAHATOYA

the flames. Next he stuffed smaller, broken branches into the heap to provide an easily combustible supply of kindling. He supplemented the kindling with armfuls of dry grass and leaves gathered from the ground. He tested the wind direction once more. It was light, almost imperceptible, but blowing in the right direction—toward the most likely position of the Nazi agent.

The sun had barely cleared the summit of West Peak but it was just enough. Michael took out his most innocuous but, right now, most important survival tool, a small magnifying glass. The tiny round glass captured the sun's rays and Michael pointed the resulting beam at the bone dry mass of fire starter. Waiting was always the hardest. A tiny sliver of smoke curled innocently around the glass piece. Michael waited patiently. He saw a spot of black appear on the dry pile and then, more smoke. The tiniest of flames flickered at the foot of the steady smoke column. Michael bent down and gently blew on the flame. It crackled and grew. He gave it more of his breath to nurture the flame. Another minute of nursing the newborn flames, and the fire took on a life of its own. It sputtered as it grew into a dangerous beast with a voracious appetite. Michael stepped back, momentarily mesmerized.

Okay, now it's done. God help us all. He set out to take up his observation position to provide backup for Agent King. A nagging uncertainty was festering in his psyche. *Is the German we assumed that Joe shot, alive or dead?* Michael hated assumptions. They could be deadly but he didn't have time to ponder his alternatives or try and determine probabilities of various scenarios. Time was running out for Sven and what was left of the crew and their VIP defector.

As a seasoned old Drill Instructor had yelled into his ear during his first training exercise as a platoon leader, "Do SOMETHING, Meathead, even if it's wrong!" Michael reminded himself that this mission was about preventing the Germans from getting their hands on a spy who knew some of America's most precious and dangerous secrets.

At first the flame whispered and demurely pranced among the dead Aspen trunks. As its appetite for the bone-dry fuel exploded, it gulped oxygen from the already thin air and then it roared. As it gained strength, it gathered speed and flames raced across the forest floor and climbed the tallest pine trees in seconds. The gentlest breeze goaded it and sped the monster further into the forest where it quickly spread. As far as wildfires go, it was almost perfect.

Brian King, sitting high in a fir tree, could see the thick billowing smoke and flames reaching for the heavens. *Oh, my God. Michael outdid himself this time.* He quickly re-focused his attention on the task of spotting the German (or Germans). Until he saw a dead body, he would assume both Germans were alive. He didn't like nasty surprises either.

Don't Play With Fire

THE WAHATOYA

119

naiku

Dietmar noticed the acrid smell in the air first. Then his eyes began to sting. The minor irritant soon became suffocating. He didn't have to see or hear the roar of the flames to know that a fire was raging nearby. Remarkably, his first thought was not how to escape, but how to position himself to survive and continue the mission. He thought that the fire would most likely flush out the Americans and give him the opportunity to kill them and grab the scientist. He quickly formulated a plan. Arndt must have been close to discovering the Americans' hiding place when he was shot. He would start there.

Brian King was about a hundred yards away when he broke out of the heavy brush. Normally, Dietmar would have left very quickly and run to the next cover, but he had been sitting in the same position for too long and his right leg had gone to sleep. He pushed off with his left leg and extended his right one to start his sprint but his right leg collapsed and he landed on his right knee, which was also numb. Brian fired, anticipating an upward and forward movement of Dietmar's torso. The round whizzed just above Dietmar's head. Brian recognized the aiming error and fired again. Dietmar had instinctively propelled himself forward with his good left leg and prepared to roll his body to present a moving target. The second shot tore through his right ankle. He felt his ankle jump from the impact of the bullet, but he didn't feel the pain because of his leg's numbness. He pushed with his left leg and pulled with his elbows to get to cover. Brian no longer had a target so he half-climbed, and half-slid from his firing position in the tree to pursue his target on foot.

The sudden, explosive movement and the adrenalin pumping through his body had returned the circulation to Dietmar's right leg and he was beginning to feel the pain. It hit him like a sledge hammer.

Dietmar knew that the shooter would be coming soon. He scrambled on his belly into a clump of bushes. He was leaving a blood trail. Dietmar had to set himself up to ambush the shooter before he was discovered. He twisted his body into a sitting position. He was now about fifteen yards from where Arndt was standing when he was shot, behind the rock outcropping, in a depression that appeared to slope down to his right. He leaned back and took deep breaths to steady himself. His ankle was afire with pain. The smoke seemed to be getting thicker and it burned his lungs. He lay his rifle down and slipped his handgun out of its holster.

naiku

Damn! The only thing worse than a Nazi bastard is a Nazi bastard you just shot but didn't kill. Damnit! Now he's a pissed off Nazi bastard. Brian chastised himself. Then he reined himself in. *Not a good idea to go busting through the brush half-cocked.* Brian knew that the German couldn't have gone very far because he had seen him crawling after he was shot. He also knew that because of the steepness of the terrain around that spot, he had very few options in approaching the once-again-hiding German. The smoke was even thicker and Brian decided that it would give him suitable cover. He crept on his belly where the smoke seemed less dense, to lower his profile. When he reached the large rock outcropping, he rose to a squatting position and hesitated. He sensed more than saw a rapid movement off his left hindquarter. He instinctively rolled forward to lessen the impact and to use the attacker's momentum to his own advantage. The force of the collision shocked him. Dietmar's lunge was slightly off-center and Brian's early movement had thrown him off even more. But it was more than a glancing blow and they both rolled forward. Brian was able to disentangle himself and scrambled to his feet with his knife in his hand. Even with a wounded ankle, Dietmar was able to stand as well and he lunged off his left foot, swinging his knife at Brian's mid-section. Brian dodged and briefly thought that this would be easy pickings for him. But even with a wounded ankle, Dietmar soon burst that bubble. He went on the offensive, swinging his knife in a series of tight arcs, first at Brian's head, then at his mid-section.

Damn, he had a knife in each hand. Brian parried, dodged and backtracked, watching for an opening. He found one when Dietmar tried a backhanded swipe. Brian deftly sliced Dietmar's right arm as it passed in front of him. The German never flinched. Then Brian played defense, waiting for his chance. When the German swung high at Brian's head, he quickly thrust his knife upward toward Dietmar's face. Dietmar swung his other arm up in a defensive maneuver. That action momentarily put his body in an overstretched posture. Brian squatted down and, using his right hand to support his body and provide a pivot point, swung his left foot with all his might and crashed it into Dietmar's bleeding ankle, sweeping it out from under him. Dietmar screamed in agony and went down hard. Brian jumped up and pounced, expecting to deliver a fatal blow with his blade. He knew Dietmar couldn't use his right foot so he stayed on that side of him. Unfortunately, Dietmar was at his best when cornered. He delivered a crushing blow with his right foot to Brian's groin. Dietmar almost fainted from the pain of delivering that blow and Brian dropped to his knees. They were both in agony, trying to recover enough strength to end the fight. Dietmar's right ankle was bleeding

THE WAHATOYA   121

profusely. He struggled to his feet. Brian tried to stand and was halfway up
when Dietmar came for him with the knife. He was too close for Brian to
dodge so he rushed the German and grabbed his knife hand to keep it away
from his body. Dietmar grunted loudly and swiveled his body, grabbing Brian's
wrist and with a mighty heave threw Brian to the ground. Brian struggled to
regain his footing but the German was just too quick and strong. *I'm about
to die*, Brian thought.

The loud *THUNK* reverberated in Dietmar's ears as he collapsed to his
knees and toppled face first onto the hard rock. Brian looked up.

"I thought you could use some help." Sven said matter of factly. He
tossed the gnarled pinón stick to the ground. Brian couldn't speak. He just
nodded and breathed deeply for a few minutes. Eventually, they moved the
unconscious German into the cave.

naiku

Even though protected from the fire raging outside, the cave was becoming
very smoky. The cave system's natural ventilation was now working against
them by sucking the smoke into the cavern. They discussed how to proceed.
Brian wanted to bundle up Daniel and start down the mountain with him.
He was the only reason they were there

Daniel ebbed in and out of a coma. If he could have voted, he would
have told his caretakers to put him out of his misery.

"Can we be sure the other German is dead?" Sven wondered.

"No," Brian replied, "but we could make a lot of progress with the smoke
hiding our movement. Michael can take care of himself if he makes it this
far and sees that we're gone."

naiku

Unfortunately, Michael couldn't tell them his own preference. He found
himself trapped between two roaring sections of the fire. The fire had gotten
so hot that it was beginning to make its own weather, sucking in a tremendous
amount of air to fuel its enormous appetite. The winds shifted constantly
and Michael couldn't see a way out. The air was thick with heat and soot.
He dropped to his knees to find better air. His lungs were beginning to feel
the effects of the heated air and the soot.

I'm going to burn to death in my own fire, he thought. He became
disoriented and began to crawl aimlessly. Something or someone bumped

into him. Someone else ran past him. *Who can that be? I must be delirious,* he thought. Then he looked up ahead and he could see a mule doe with two fawns running ahead of him. He could feel the earth vibrate with more footsteps. It took him a minute to realize the significance of the parade of wildlife. They knew the way out!

He got to his feet and quickened his pace in the direction of the fleeing deer. The intensity of the heat soon abated and he relaxed a little but kept moving. He was coughing up black goop by now. The smoke thinned out some and he was able to get his bearings. *If I can make it to the waterfall, I'll be safe.* He allowed himself a bit of hope. He used landmarks that Lonnie Dunn had described to orient himself. West Peak loomed large, stoically presiding over the fiery mayhem. Michael trudged through the smoke. He could see flames climbing a large Ponderosa pine. They threw off a shower of glowing embers. Michael could hear the roar of Chaparral Falls. The thick smoke helped hide him so he wasn't as cautious as he approached Joe Cordova's hiding spot.

Joe wasn't there. *Maybe the fire spooked him and he moved,* Michael thought. But he could see where Joe had been sitting. The grass was laid flat. He walked in a circle around the spot, looking for signs of Joe's movement. Instead, he found a bleeding and barely breathing Joe. Michael knelt on one knee.

"Joe, can you hear me?" Michael whispered, his body tense. This was obviously the work of one of the Germans.

Joe opened his eyes. "The sneaky bastard got me from behind. I . . . . didn't see . . ." His voice trailed off. Joe's breathing was shallow and irregular. Michael checked his pulse. It was rapid and weak. Joe was barely alive. He tried to continue. "I'm . . . . I . . . . sorry."

"Don't worry my friend. We've got things under control," Michael lied. He raised his head and scanned the terrain. The smoke made it impossible to see beyond about twenty feet. His gaze fell on the waterfall. The German probably spotted Joe's position and figured out Joe was guarding the back entrance to Sven's hiding place. Michael considered his next move. It seemed likely that the German would have entered the cave looking for their defector if he had gotten this close. *Where's the other Nazi? Is one of them wounded? Where's Brian King?* Michael knew that three shots had been fired, all by expert marksmen. That meant the chances were excellent that at least one, and maybe both, of the enemy were wounded. Brian King's position or condition was unknown. Joe was out of the picture. Sven and the others were supposedly in the cave. Michael was used to dealing with uncertainty. Every field operation was full of them. No question about it, he needed to go into the cave, hopefully without

THE WAHATOYA

123

being detected. Flames were all around him. He couldn't leave Joe out here alone. Michael knelt down again and hoisted Joe up over his shoulder. He was still alive, but barely.

Michael waded into the waist-deep pool and carried Joe to the base of the falls. He heaved Joe up and pushed him through the falling water. Then he pulled himself up on to the ledge and crawled through the waterfall. Michael crawled over Joe and pulled him into the cave's dark entrance.

"Sorry, Joe, I've got to leave you here for a while."

The Nazi, Arndt, rose to his feet behind a thick tangle of bushes. *So that's where they are.* He had been patiently waiting and watching since ambushing Joe several hours earlier. He thought he had killed him. *Oh well, they'll all be dead soon enough.* After taking Joe's bullet through his collar bone, he had applied a very crude bandage to the wound and had tied his arm with a makeshift sling. Michael's fire had, indeed, been unexpected. The Americans were usually not so creative. *No matter*, he thought, *the end result will be the same.* He headed down the steep bank toward the waterfall, holding his injured right arm close to his side.

Agent King helped Sven carry the motionless Dietmar through the hidden entrance. Brian had tied his hands behind him and bound his feet tightly. He knew how dangerous the Nazi was. *What a catch*, he thought. *If we can deliver live Nazi spies to our intel guys in Washington, they'll pee all over themselves.* They dumped him on the hard floor. His limp body slumped against the wall. He lay on his side in a crumpled pile. Brian got his first look at Daniel.

Brian exclaimed, "My god, what happened to his leg?"

Sven responded matter-of-factly, "I had to amputate it. I don't think he's going to be much use to the Germans."

Brian turned his gaze to Ben Curtis. "Are you the pilot?"

"Well, I used to be the pilot. I'm terribly sorry about the other agents." Brian had not been sure of the fate of the others, but had a pretty good idea, as did they all, that the agents were dead. Brian looked at Ben's face, taking measure of him. Ben was a mere shadow of the once proud air warrior and hero of Polesti. He was physically, mentally and emotionally exhausted. Ben knew in his heart of hearts that he had done his best but he could not shake the crushing guilt and remorse. Every pilot who had ever flown in command of an airplane knew that the mission, the crew and the passengers were ultimately his responsibility. The old saying, "You can delegate authority but you can never delegate responsibility" rang through Ben's soul. Brian King had served in the military and he knew exactly what Ben was going through. He extended his hand and shook Ben's.

"This is one bitch of a mission but we're going to make it." He nodded his head toward the unconscious Dietmar and said, "One down, one to go."

Brian turned his head and motioned quiet. He listened—*Click-click, click-click-click.* He reached inside his shirt and pulled out a small metal object hanging around his neck. He answered—*Click-click-click, click-click.* They had borrowed the clicker-mode of identification from the D-Day invasion forces.

Michael soon appeared, dripping from his watery entrance. "Joe Cordova is badly hurt. He's lying by the waterfall, just inside the cave entrance." Ben and Sven hurried to get him. Michael stared at Dietmar. "Just him?" he questioned Brian in his "Oh-Shit" tone.

"Yeah, why?" Brian readied his automatic weapon. Michael closed his eyes. "I think I just showed his buddy where we are."

Michael just realized that Sven and Ben were in great danger if the German was coming in behind him. He was about to head that way and call them back when he heard a muffled scream of pain.

Without a word, Michael and Brian split up. They had to keep the German guessing. He didn't know how many of them were in the cave other than Michael. Michael ducked into a short passageway that led to a small room to the right. Brian moved quickly beyond that room and found a pile of rubble to hide behind. He was completely out of sight.

Sven came into the dim light first. Ben followed and Arndt was close behind, holding the sharp point of a large blade tight against Ben's throat, piercing his skin. His neck was oozing blood. Arndt was holding the knife in his good hand and had his good arm wrapped around Ben's neck and held him close. It was awkward, but effective. Arndt spotted Dietmar and ordered Sven to cut him loose.

Michael knew that he was the one that had to confront the Nazi, because Arndt had seen him enter the cave. Arndt did not know that Brian King was here also. They needed to keep him guessing about their forces. Surprise was their best weapon against such a well trained enemy. Michael wanted to get close to him. He stepped out from the dark.

"Let him go. We'll give you your spy. He's no use to us anymore, and he's going to die before you get him to Deutschland," Michael lied to distract him.

"Drop your weapon. I'll take our man and kill all of you as well," Arndt spewed hatred. Michael lay down his pistol. He could see out of the corner of his eye that Dietmar was beginning to come around as Sven cut his bindings. Daniel was up on one elbow. He began to sob.

"Oh Dear God."

THE WAHATOYA   125

"You pathetic traitor," Arndt shot the words at Daniel. His face was distorted with rage. Daniel couldn't comprehend what was happening. Tears poured down his face. His soul was in agony and he was helpless. *What had he done?*

Brian saw Michael move from his hiding place. Brian slipped out of the dark room, pressing his body tightly against the wall as he crept closer. Brian cradled his pistol. He knew what Michael was expecting. Brian needed to distract Arndt so that Michael could move quickly. He knew that Michael would try to get close to Arndt so Brian had to be very precise if he used his weapon. Brian was close now. Just around one dark corner, and he would be able to see the German. He wouldn't have time to assess the situation.

Michael's internal clock was telling him that Brian would have moved into position by now. He took a step.

"Listen, we can help you get out of the country. Our government will be very embarrassed about all of this and will want to keep it quiet. I can guarantee your safe passage." Michael took another small step. Arndt shifted his body slightly as he turned to keep Ben between himself and Michael. Ben was sweating profusely. Arndt's arm was cocked around Ben's neck and he was still holding the blade at his neck.

Arndt's face was red. He screamed at Michael, "You stupid American. I'm going to kill all of you!" He rotated the knife so that the razor sharp blade was placed to cut Ben's throat.

Brian stepped out of the darkness. The blast of his forty-five automatic split the air like a cannon. It bounced off the walls of the cave. The muzzle blast momentarily blinded everyone but Michael, who had averted his eyes. Ben felt like the new secret bomb had exploded against his shoulder. He and Arndt flew backward and slammed into the cave wall. Ben's body went limp and Arndt couldn't hold up Ben's weight with his one good arm. Michael was on him in an instant and pulled Ben's body out of Arndt's grasp. Brian was right behind Michael and caught Ben as Michael flung him to one side. The forty-five round had hit Ben in the right shoulder and exited into Arndt's chest, not far below his shattered clavicle. Yes, FBI Agent Brian King had shot the hostage. Arndt screamed in pain. His front was covered with blood. To Michael's surprise, Arndt twisted his body to the left, just enough to wrest his body away from Michael's grasp. Michael remembered the knife and sucked in his mid-section just in time to avoid being sliced by Arndt's arcing blade. Arndt screamed again as the pain of the twisting movement almost overcame him.

Michael had recovered and he delivered an explosive kick to Arndt's jaw. The force sent the German hard against the cave wall. He kicked out at

Michael, who caught the heel of Arndt's boot on his shin and lost his balance. Arndt scrambled to his knees and launched himself on top of Michael. He had lost the knife, but held his pistol to Michael's head. Both of them were gasping for air and Arndt was bleeding profusely from his newest bullet wound. Michael's chest was heaving. He prepared himself to die. The German pointed the pistol at Brian King while he held Michael's neck with his knee and pressed down, cutting off Michael's air.

"Move over there," Arndt screamed at Brian as he waved his pistol to his right. "Drop your pistol now." Brian laid it on the ground and moved as directed. They were in a hell of a fix with this crazy Nazi. Dietmar was coming to and would join his comrade soon.

"Hey, Herr German." Sven appeared from the dark. "Let him go and I'll show you the gold."

Arndt looked puzzled. *What gold? They told me nothing about gold.*

Arndt blinked the sweat out of his eyes and began to recover his faculties. With his gun still aimed at Brian, he looked at Sven. Sven stared back. He was beyond being intimidated by a German thug. Sven had a great card and he was going to play it.

"What will Hitler think, when he learns that you missed a fortune in gold that you could've brought back with your spy. Hell, he's gonna die on you anyway. Wouldn't it be nice to bring Der Fuhrer a consolation prize?"

Arndt stood up shakily, still pointing his gun at Brian. He motioned Michael to get up and join Brian.

"Where is your gold?"

"It's in this cave, in the back."

Arndt had them in a tight cluster, controlling them with his one good arm and his pistol. Michael didn't know what Sven was planning but he knew that Arndt couldn't hold out much longer. Then Dietmar regained consciousness and Arndt rattled off a barrage of German to him. Sven and Brian had stripped him of his weapons when they brought him into the cave.

Sven lit a torch to light the way and show Arndt the gold. It took a few minutes because Arndt was suspicious. They finally arrived at a room full of old, worn leather satchels stacked as high as a man's head.

"Here it is. See for yourself." Sven pulled one of the satchels off its perch and it thumped to the floor. He bent down, undid the clasp and kicked open the satchel. The gold Spanish coins spilled out onto the hard rock floor. Sven held the torch down close.

The old man tells the truth. Arndt's mind raced. *What a find!* If he could get this gold back to Germany, he would be honored by Hitler. It never occurred

THE WAHATOYA

127

to him that he might stay in the United States with it. Everything revolved around the Father Land. *How on earth will we move it, though?*

As Sven had planned, the German was distracted by this unexpected development. Sven couldn't risk attacking the German. He eased himself to a position directly in front of the satchels and ran his hand along the top of the stack. He found the rope that he had placed there years ago.

"Herr German, you need to see this." Sven motioned to the top of the satchels. "This is the best part of all." Arndt held the gun on Sven and moved closer. Sven yanked hard on the rope, which dislodged a row of wooden stanchions. The supporting beams collapsed and unleashed a river of large rocks, which came thundering down through a natural channel. A crushing mass of rocks crashed onto the satchels of gold, burying everything and everyone in the room. The falling rocks shook the ground and sent a cloud of dust whooshing through the corridors of the cave. Sven and the German died as their rock grave settled about them.

naiku

When Towaoc was on his death bed, he had made Sven promise to never let the gold coins be used for evil. He told him to use them for a good and noble cause and if such a use never presented itself to make sure that the coins stayed hidden forever. Sven had fulfilled his promise. Besides, it was a good day to die.

"Earthquake!" Michael yelled at the top of his lungs. Dietmar, startled by the trembling earth and the roar of the crashing rocks, turned his head. Michael rushed him and knocked him to the ground. The German fired point blank at Michael. The bullet tore through his side. He clutched the wound as Dietmar rolled him to the side. Brian dove for his rifle. The German fired twice. A bullet smashed Brian's elbow. His arm exploded in pain and then went numb. He grabbed his arm and rolled over to avoid yet another round from the German's pistol. Click. The German fired point blank at Brian's head but the gun was now empty.

"Hey, you Nazi bastard!" Ben yelled at him. The angry Dietmar was in a killing frenzy and turned to Ben, whose wounded right arm hung at his side. He reached down into the smoldering campfire with his left hand and scooped up a handful of hot ash and coals and flung them directly into the Nazi's crazed eyes.

Dietmar screamed hysterically and tried to brush his face clean. Ben had never heard such screams of pain. Dietmar ran into the cave wall. His screams turned into unintelligible grunts and sputtering. Ben looked around for a weapon. His hand was blistered and red and he wanted to scream, too.

No Greater Love

Damn, that hurts! The German was on his knees with his face in his hands, blubbering in German. Suddenly, he jumped to his feet and turned. He couldn't see clearly but he rushed toward Ben, catching him off guard. The Nazi was in a frenzy. He began hitting Ben with his bare hands, screaming at the top of his lungs. Ben tried to ward off the blows. Most of them struck him in the shoulders, some on the face. He felt his lip split and tasted blood. His only chance was to escape. Ben backed up while trying to protect himself. The blows that connected were fearsome and Ben feared being knocked unconscious. That would be his end. Ben began kicking, and connected a few blows himself but the German was neither deterred nor did he slow down. Ben fell to his knees. Suddenly, the German's momentum changed. Ben felt a jostle and the German let up momentarily. Dietmar was struggling. Ben scrambled backwards to escape.

"Oh, my God!" Ben could see Daniel latched onto the German's back, his arms squeezing Dietmar's neck, his remaining leg wrapped around the German's waist. Daniel, using Brian King's rifle as a crutch, had staggered over to help Ben. When Dietmar had bent down to pull Ben up from his knees, Daniel took the opportunity to launch himself onto Dietmar's back. He was squeezing Dietmar's neck as hard as he could, trying to choke the life out of him. Dietmar swung him around and slammed into the wall in a desperate attempt to dislodge his surprise assailant. Daniel screamed as his bloody stump struck the wall. But the German was growing tired too; his frenetic attack on Ben had taken its toll. Daniel would not, could not, be dislodged. Dietmar directed his anger back at Ben. He wanted to squeeze the life out of him, then he would worry about the crazy Jew clinging to his back. Ben backed toward the waterfall exit. The German rushed him and they all went flying through the falls, into the pool of water outside the cave. Ben was under Dietmar, under water, struggling to free himself before his lungs burst.

Yea, though I walk through the valley of the shadow of death, I will fear no evil.

Daniel used every ounce of strength he could summon to choke Dietmar harder and harder. Sparks and burning branches rained down on the water's surface. Ben was panicking, his lungs were bursting, he was getting light headed. *I've got to have air!* Daniel willed himself to hold his breath and bear down all his weight to keep the thrashing German's head under water. Dietmar was starving for air. He released Ben and tried to stand up but Daniel's weight on his back was too far forward. The German couldn't get his feet on the bottom of the pool or raise his head out of the water. Daniel squeezed harder. He would never let go. Never. Ben was coughing up water and gasping for air. He splashed his way to Daniel and pulled him off the German's back.

Can't Keep a Good Man Down

THE WAHATOYA

131

"Daniel, come on Daniel." He dragged Daniel's lifeless body to the bank and pushed him on to dry land with his good arm. He tried desperately to revive him but Daniel was gone—at last freed from his personal demons and his guilt by a sacrificial act of atonement.

Ben verified that Dietmar was dead. He returned to the cave and found Agent King and Michael and bandaged their gunshot wounds. Together they carried Joe Cordova outside. He had a serious head injury but would survive. Ben surveyed the mound of rubble, under which Sven and the German were buried. He decided not to try and dig them out. Ben suspected that Sven had been responsible for pulling the rocks down on both of them and that he was at peace. If the U.S. government wanted the German's body, he would leave it up to them to come and dig him out.

The Wahatoya's most spectacular geological feature had subdued the fire. The blaze had burned right up to one of the dikes that radiated out from the peaks. These natural rock walls provided a barrier to the fire's progress and it went out with a smoky whimper.

naiku

Twelve hours earlier reinforcements had arrived in force in La Veta. Sheriff Lonnie Dunn had never seen so many armed men with so much fire power. Grim and efficient, the FBI agents and Army Rangers blocked off streets around the Sheriff's office and imposed a war-like atmosphere on the sleepy rural town. *Well, so much for stealth*, Sheriff Dunn mused. He briefed them on the last known position of Michael and Agent King and showed them where the cave was located and where Joe Cordova had been situated. By the time they got to the meadow near the canyon's entrance, the fire was sputtering. The colonel in charge of the recovery force sent out three soldiers to assess the fire's scope and direction of movement. Fortunately, the fire was in its death throes by this time. Three groups set out with Sheriff Dunn leading the direct assault team. Two other teams flanked the cave from the left and the right. These teams scoured the surrounding forest for any signs of additional enemy forces. These men took the threat of Germans on U.S. soil very seriously.

Sheriff Dunn's team arrived at the water fall first. Ben assured them that the two Germans were dead. Medics treated Agent King's and Michael's injuries and examined Joe Cordova. Ben led a small group into the cave and showed them where the two bodies were buried. They immediately set up a work

Watery Inferno

THE WAHATOYA   133

crew to recover the German's remains. Ben told Sheriff Dunn about Sven's sacrifice. Lonnie told the Colonel that he thought it would be appropriate to leave Sven's body where it lay. They found Arndt's body without much trouble but the satchels of gold coins were left to be discovered another time.

"I'll get in touch with Sven's son and let him decide on the final disposition," Lonnie told him.

The Germans' bodies were wrapped and readied for transport to the morgue in La Veta. A recovery team started out for the site of the B-24 crash to recover those bodies.

Ben told them everything about Daniel's dilemma, his injury, Sven's surgery and Daniel's sacrifice to save Ben's life. Ben broke down. It all came crashing down on him. His own wounds had taken their toll on him. The medics insisted that he be hospitalized as soon as he got to Pueblo.

naiku

Two weeks later, Steven Curry, Sven's son, brought his wife and their two children, Lane, aged four, and Becky, aged two, to say good bye to Sven. The Army had kept the cave under guard for a week. Sheriff Dunn had travelled to the Ute Reservation to tell Steven in person that his father was dead. Steven wanted to talk to Ben about Sven's last days. It proved to be very therapeutic for Ben to relive those days on the mountain and to express to Sven's son how Sven had saved his and Daniel's life and then made the ultimate sacrifice for all of them. Ben wept as he told the story. He told Steven how lovingly Sven had talked about Steven's mother, Lily and their time living with the Utes and later their life together in his family's home in the Cuchara Valley. Ben told him what he knew about the cave behind the water fall.

Sheriff Dunn later took Steven and his family to the cave. They carried lanterns to light the dark corridors leading them to Sven's tomb. Lonnie left them at Sven's grave. Steven said a short prayer. His son Lane placed a bouquet of Mountain Lilies on the rocky grave and patted one of the larger stones.

"Bye, bye Papa."

Final Farewell

Epilogue

Soon afterward, Steven and his family moved into Sven's house near the Cuchara River. Steven had been growing restless on the reservation and he wanted to give his children a better opportunity than what the reservation offered. He threw himself into restoring and improving the old farm house. Later the family moved to Texas where Steven pursued a career in the oil fields and started a successful drilling company. After retiring, he brought his family back to Cuchara for extended vacations.

Ben Curtis was hospitalized and underwent extensive psychiatric treatment. He was able to return to flying after two years of treatment and eventually rose to the rank of general. Whether it was his head injury or the trauma of the crash on West Peak and the aftermath at Chaparral Falls, no one can say, but he lost all memory of ever being in the Wahatoya. There was no way of knowing that he would one day suffer another tragic loss in the Cuchara Valley and be reunited with Sven's heirs and the ghosts of Chaparral Falls.